GREEN LANTERN

THE ANIMATED SERIES ™

STONE ARCH BOOKS
a capstone imprint

▼▼ STONE ARCH BOOKS™

Published in 2013
A Capstone Imprint
1710 Roe Crest Drive
North Mankato, MN 56003
www.capstonepub.com

DC Comics
1700 Broadway, New York, NY 10019
A Warner Bros. Entertainment Company

Cataloging-in-Publication Data is available at the
Library of Congress website:
ISBN: 978-1-4342-5566-2 (library binding)

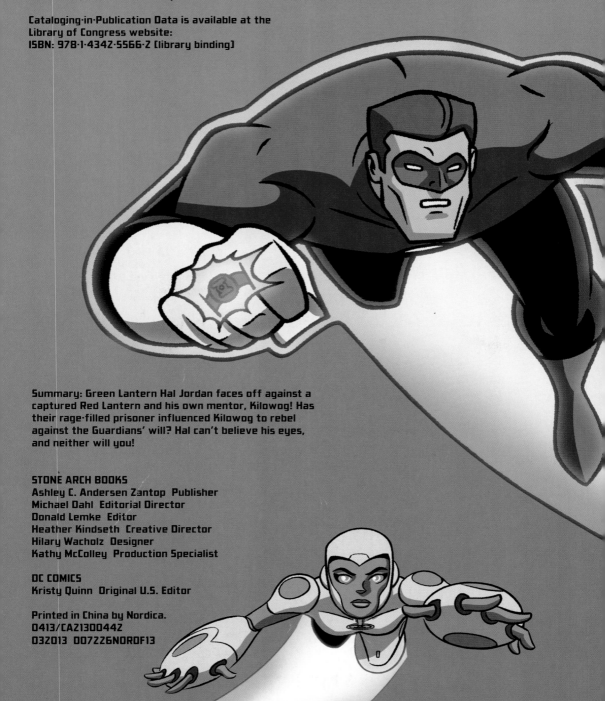

Summary: Green Lantern Hal Jordan faces off against a
captured Red Lantern and his own mentor, Kilowog! Has
their rage-filled prisoner influenced Kilowog to rebel
against the Guardians' will? Hal can't believe his eyes,
and neither will you!

STONE ARCH BOOKS
Ashley C. Andersen Zantop Publisher
Michael Dahl Editorial Director
Donald Lemke Editor
Heather Kindseth Creative Director
Hilary Wacholz Designer
Kathy McColley Production Specialist

DC COMICS
Kristy Quinn Original U.S. Editor

Printed in China by Nordica.
0413/CA21300442
032013 007226NORDF13

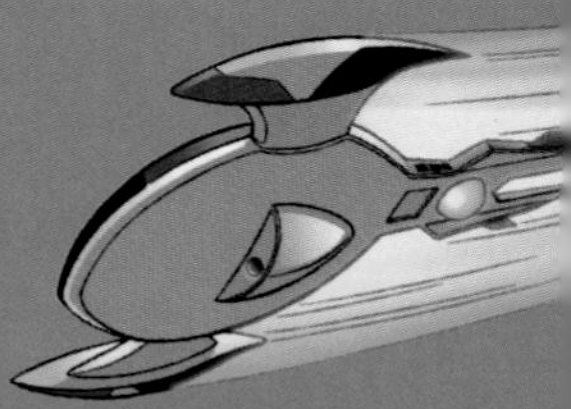

GREEN LANTERN

THE ANIMATED SERIES™

COUNTERFEITS

Art Baltazar & Franco.....................writers
Dario Brizuela............................illustrator
Gabe Eltaeb & Dario Brizuela.....colorists
Saida Abbott ....letterer

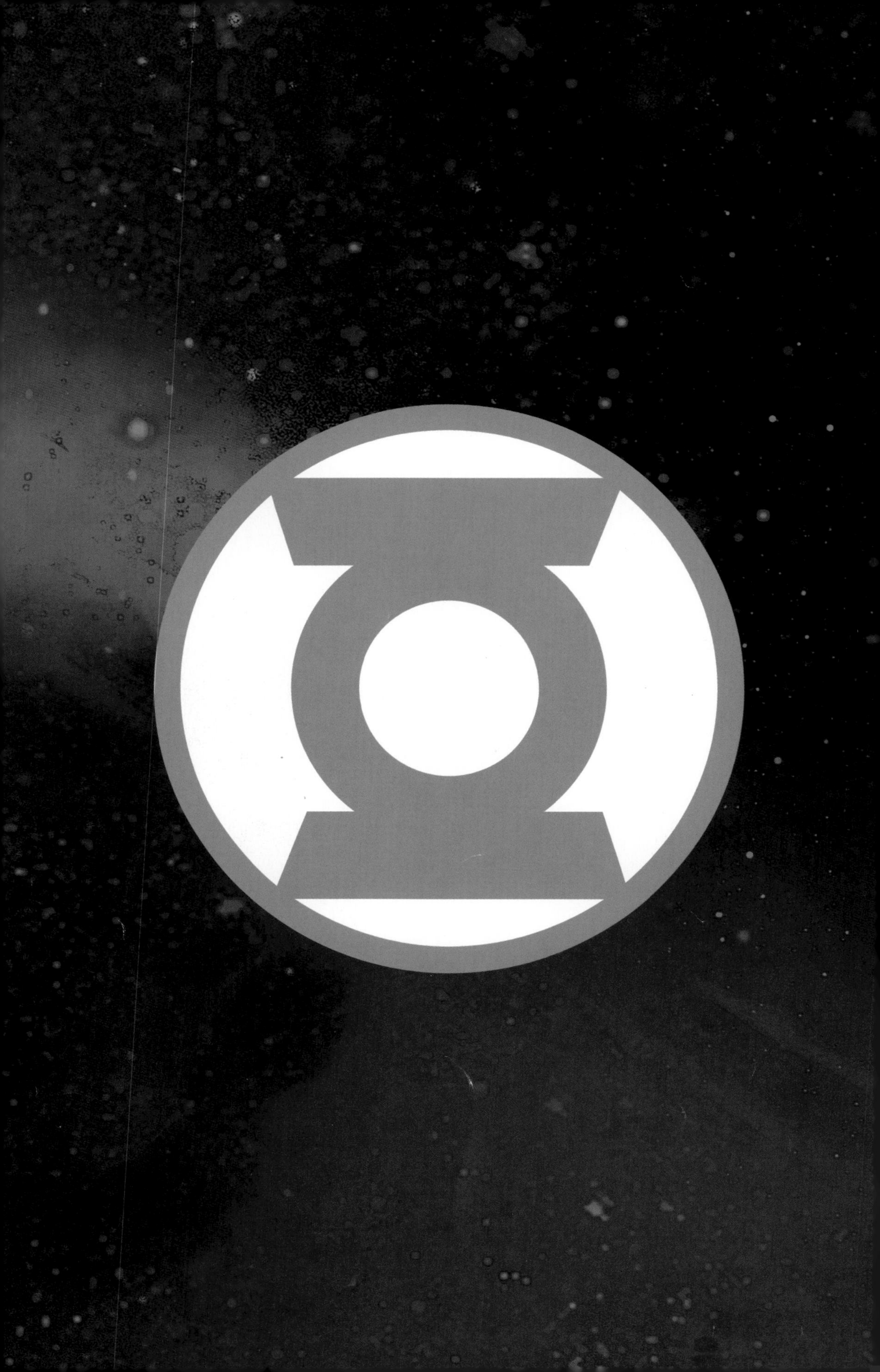

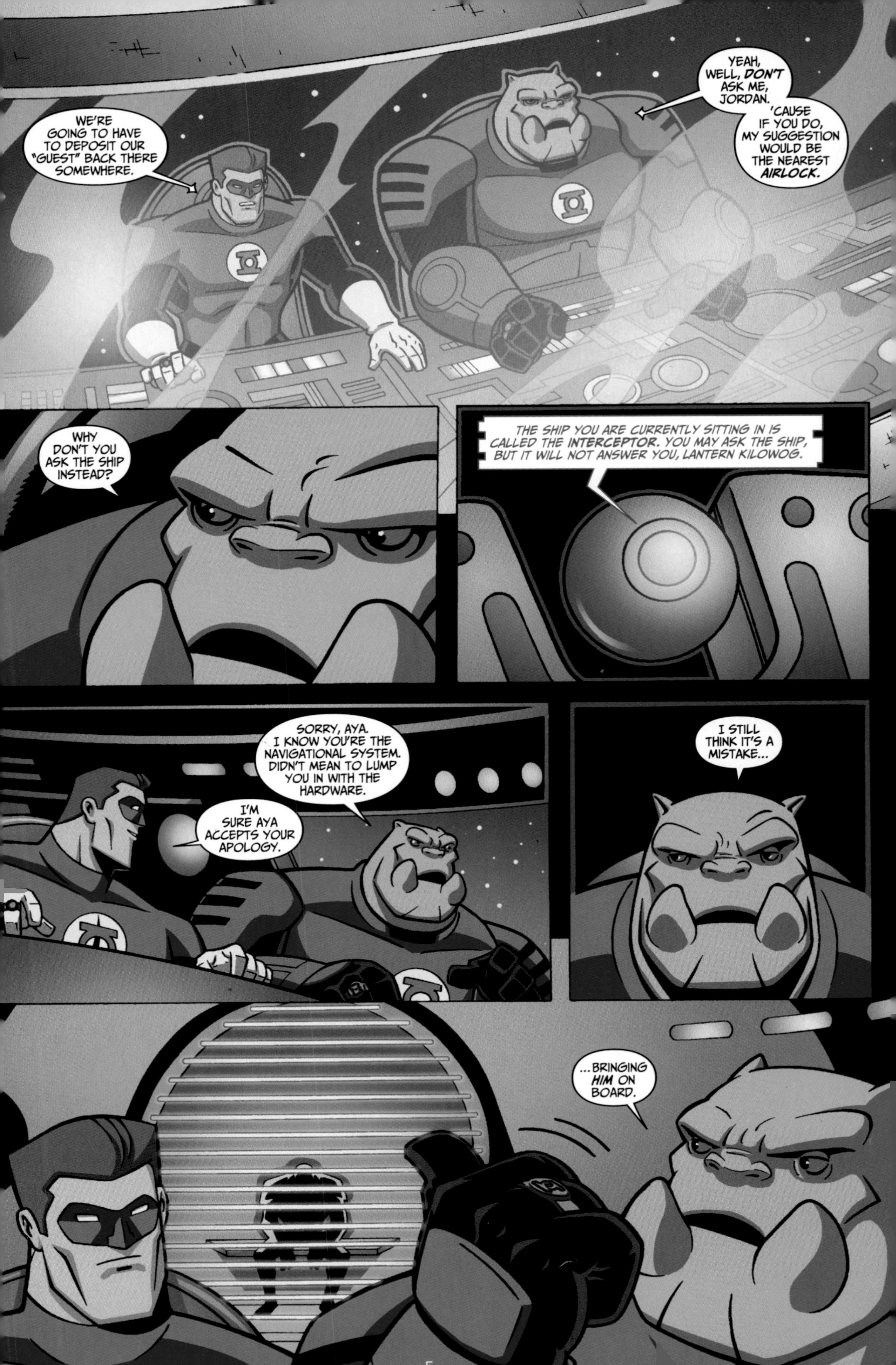
WE'RE GOING TO HAVE TO DEPOSIT OUR "GUEST" BACK THERE SOMEWHERE.
YEAH, WELL, DON'T ASK ME, JORDAN.
'CAUSE IF YOU DO, MY SUGGESTION WOULD BE THE NEAREST AIRLOCK.
WHY DON'T YOU ASK THE SHIP INSTEAD?
THE SHIP YOU ARE CURRENTLY SITTING IN IS CALLED THE INTERCEPTOR. YOU MAY ASK THE SHIP, BUT IT WILL NOT ANSWER YOU, LANTERN KILOWOG.
I'M SURE AYA ACCEPTS YOUR APOLOGY.
SORRY, AYA. I KNOW YOU'RE THE NAVIGATIONAL SYSTEM. DIDN'T MEAN TO LUMP YOU IN WITH THE HARDWARE.
I STILL THINK IT'S A MISTAKE...
...BRINGING HIM ON BOARD.

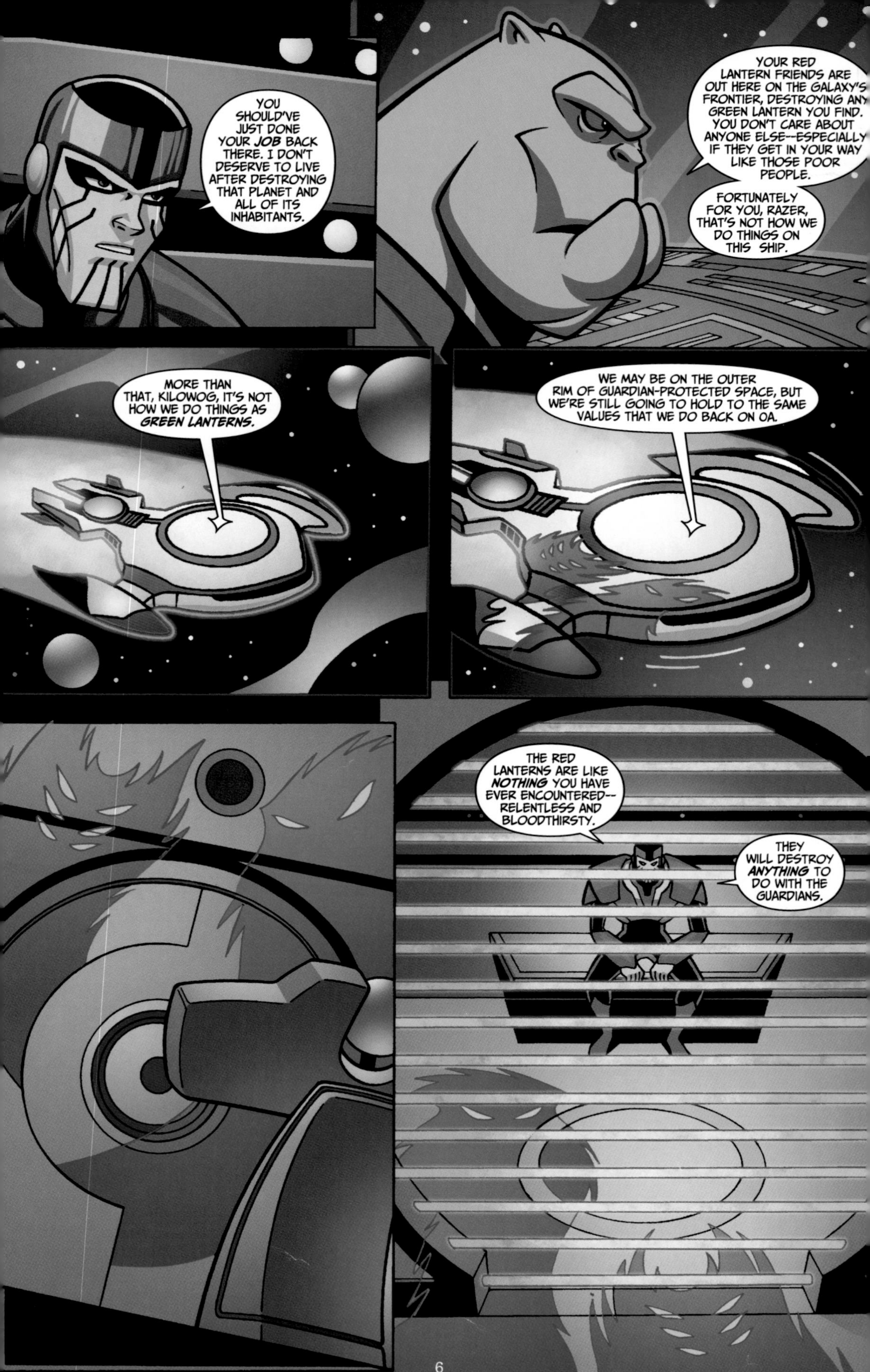

YOU SHOULD'VE JUST DONE YOUR JOB BACK THERE. I DON'T DESERVE TO LIVE AFTER DESTROYING THAT PLANET AND ALL OF ITS INHABITANTS.
YOUR RED LANTERN FRIENDS ARE OUT HERE ON THE GALAXY'S FRONTIER, DESTROYING ANY GREEN LANTERN YOU FIND. YOU DON'T CARE ABOUT ANYONE ELSE--ESPECIALLY IF THEY GET IN YOUR WAY LIKE THOSE POOR PEOPLE.
FORTUNATELY FOR YOU, RAZER, THAT'S NOT HOW WE DO THINGS ON THIS SHIP.
MORE THAN THAT, KILOWOG, IT'S NOT HOW WE DO THINGS AS GREEN LANTERNS.
WE MAY BE ON THE OUTER RIM OF GUARDIAN-PROTECTED SPACE, BUT WE'RE STILL GOING TO HOLD TO THE SAME VALUES THAT WE DO BACK ON OA.
THE RED LANTERNS ARE LIKE NOTHING YOU HAVE EVER ENCOUNTERED--RELENTLESS AND BLOODTHIRSTY.
THEY WILL DESTROY ANYTHING TO DO WITH THE GUARDIANS.

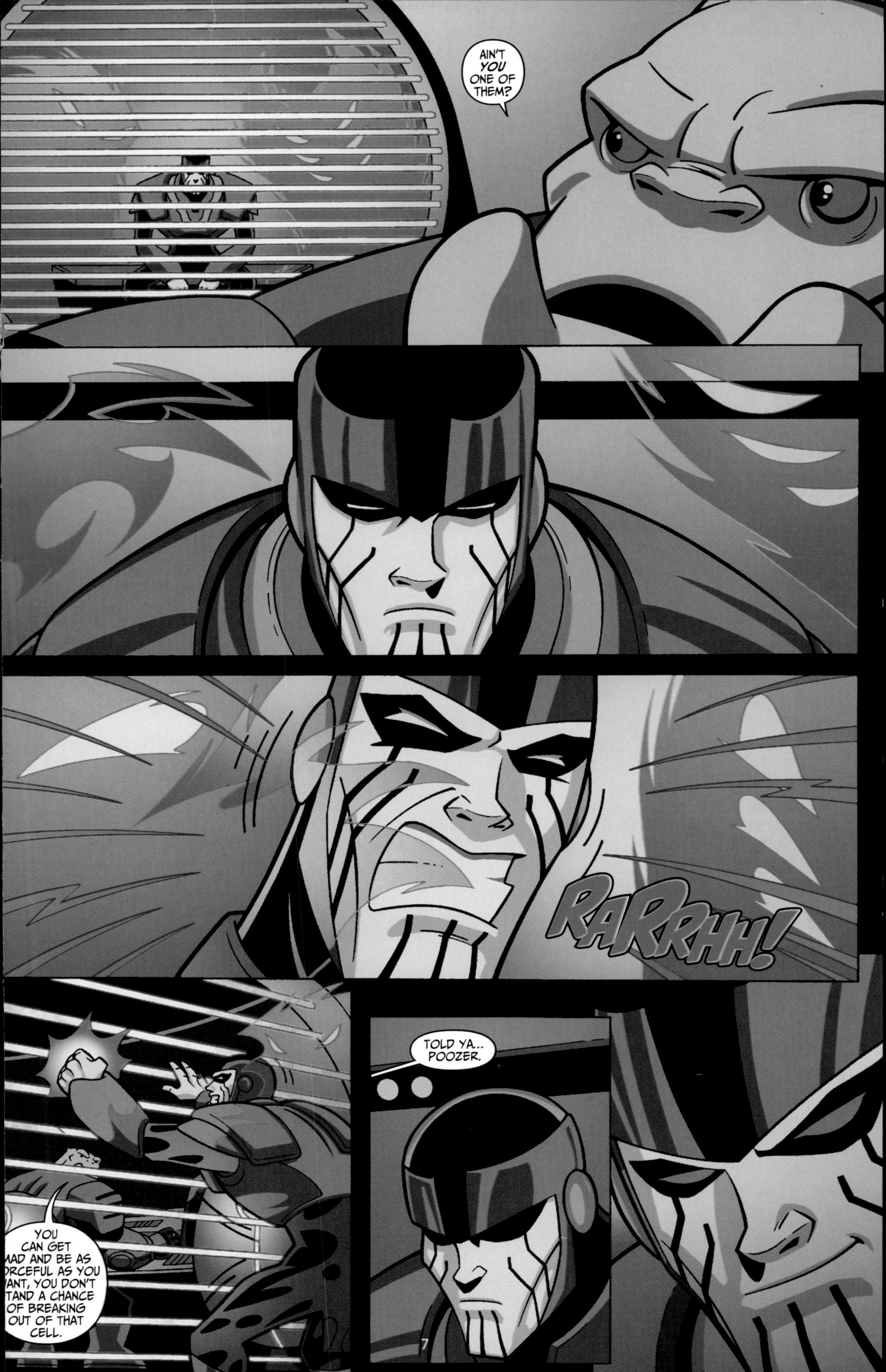
AIN'T YOU ONE OF THEM?
RARRHH!
YOU CAN GET MAD AND BE AS FORCEFUL AS YOU WANT, YOU DON'T STAND A CHANCE OF BREAKING OUT OF THAT CELL.
TOLD YA... POOZER.

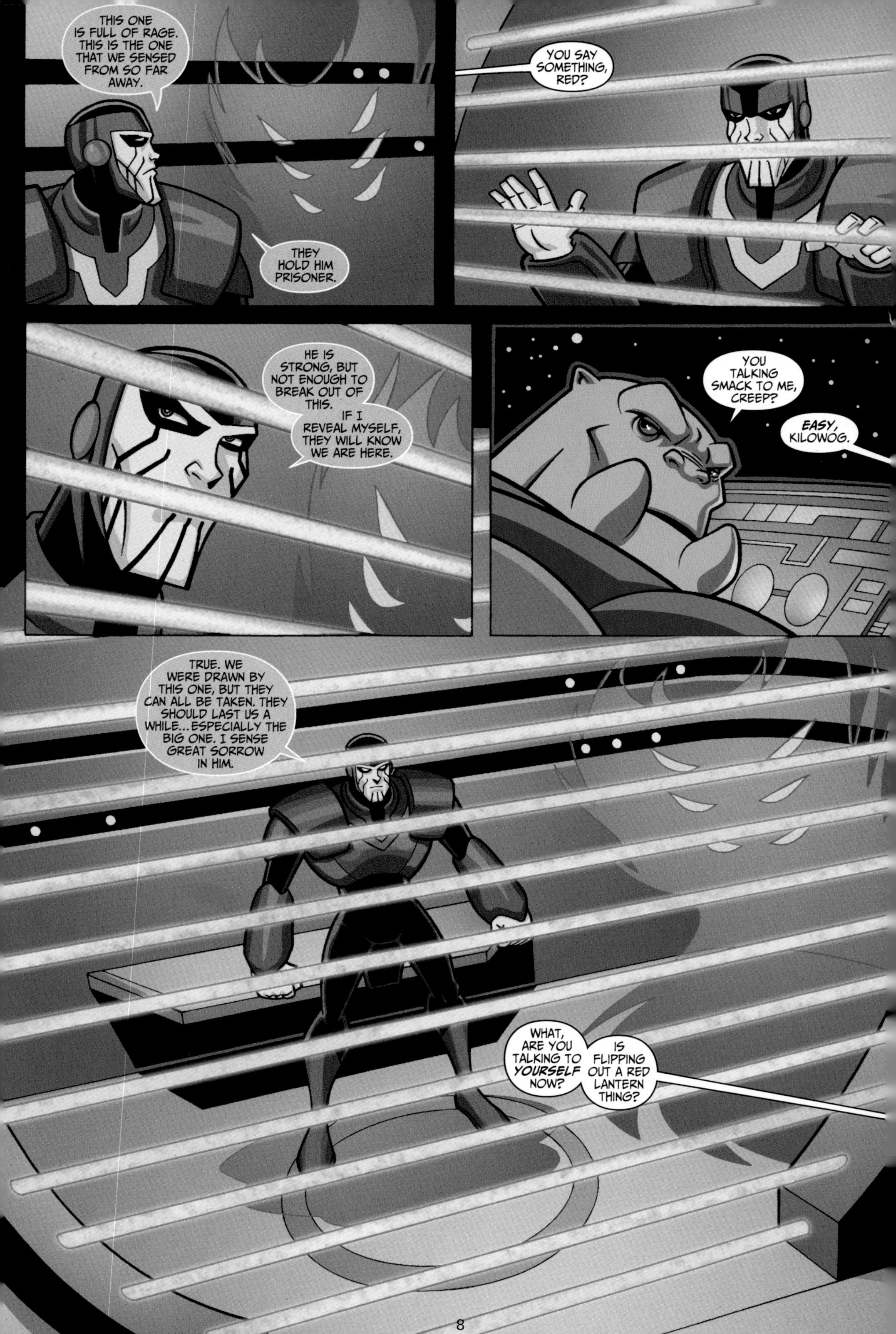

THIS ONE IS FULL OF RAGE. THIS IS THE ONE THAT WE SENSED FROM SO FAR AWAY.
THEY HOLD HIM PRISONER.
YOU SAY SOMETHING, RED?
HE IS STRONG, BUT NOT ENOUGH TO BREAK OUT OF THIS.
IF I REVEAL MYSELF, THEY WILL KNOW WE ARE HERE.
YOU TALKING SMACK TO ME, CREEP?
EASY, KILOWOG.
TRUE. WE WERE DRAWN BY THIS ONE, BUT THEY CAN ALL BE TAKEN. THEY SHOULD LAST US A WHILE...ESPECIALLY THE BIG ONE. I SENSE GREAT SORROW IN HIM.
WHAT, ARE YOU TALKING TO YOURSELF NOW?
IS FLIPPING OUT A RED LANTERN THING?

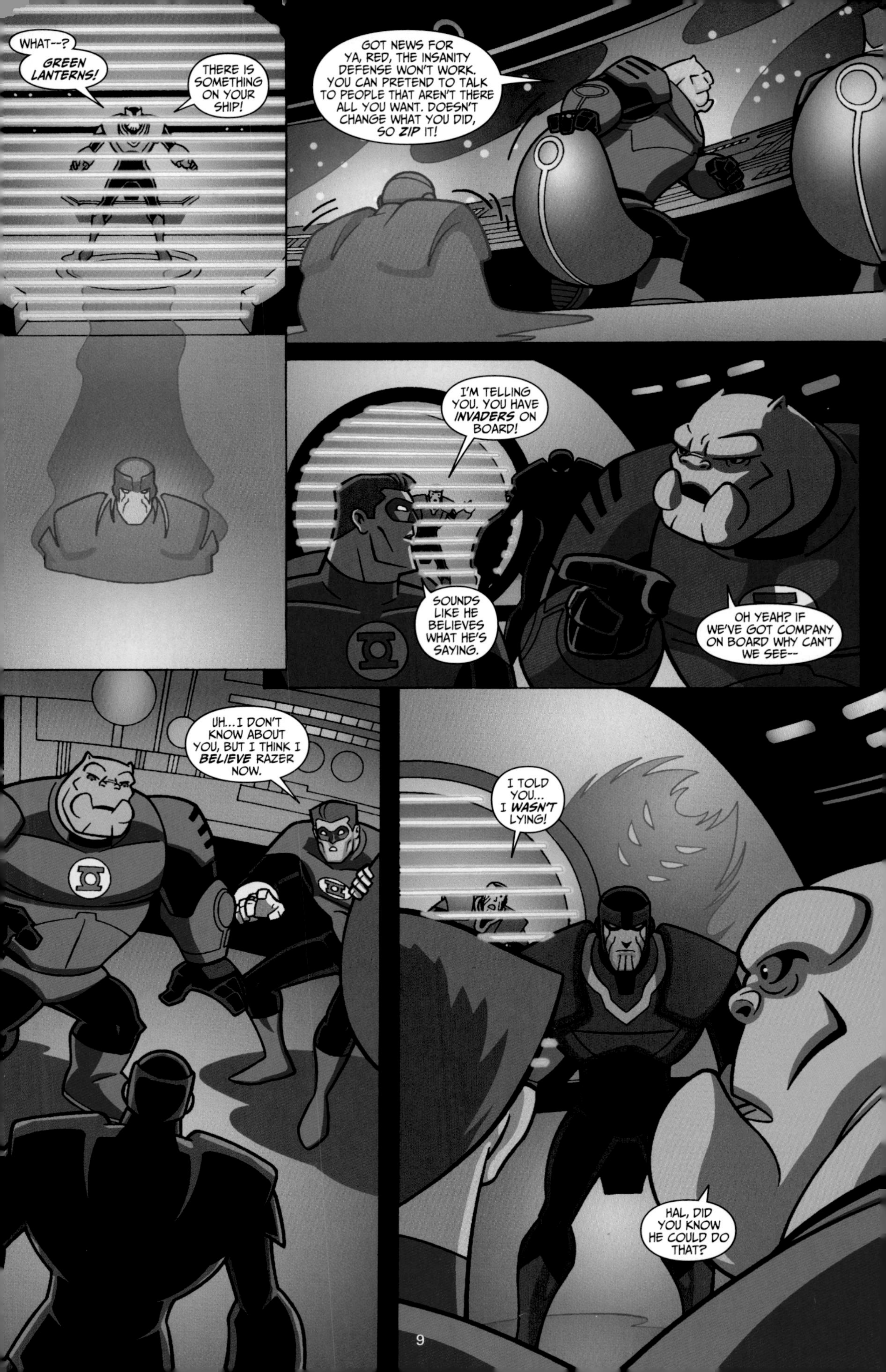
WHAT--? GREEN LANTERNS!
THERE IS SOMETHING ON YOUR SHIP!
GOT NEWS FOR YA, RED, THE INSANITY DEFENSE WON'T WORK. YOU CAN PRETEND TO TALK TO PEOPLE THAT AREN'T THERE ALL YOU WANT. DOESN'T CHANGE WHAT YOU DID, SO ZIP IT!
I'M TELLING YOU. YOU HAVE INVADERS ON BOARD!
SOUNDS LIKE HE BELIEVES WHAT HE'S SAYING.
OH YEAH? IF WE'VE GOT COMPANY ON BOARD WHY CAN'T WE SEE--
UH... I DON'T KNOW ABOUT YOU, BUT I THINK I BELIEVE RAZER NOW.
I TOLD YOU... I WASN'T LYING!
HAL, DID YOU KNOW HE COULD DO THAT?

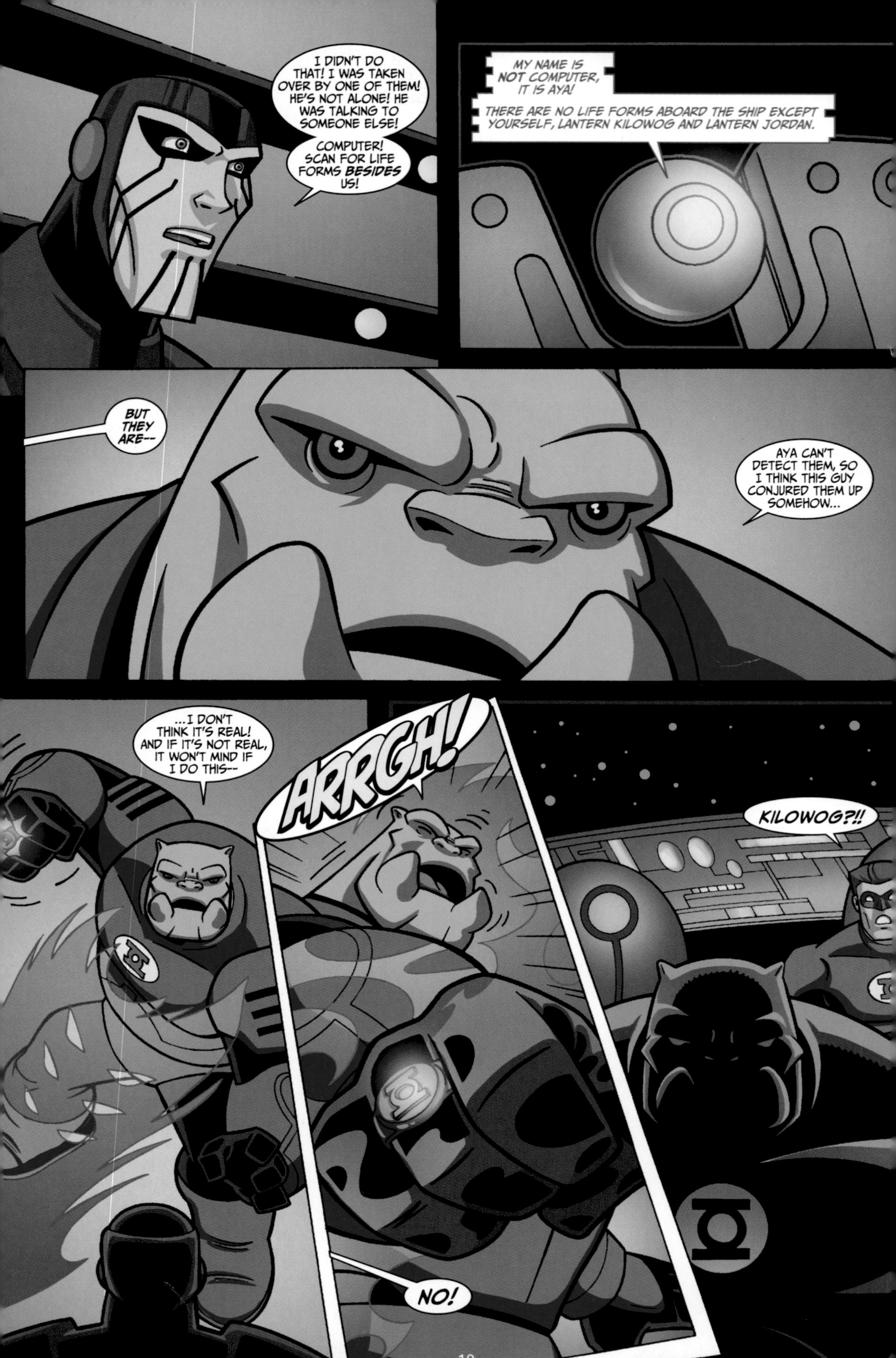

I DIDN'T DO THAT! I WAS TAKEN OVER BY ONE OF THEM! HE'S NOT ALONE! HE WAS TALKING TO SOMEONE ELSE!
COMPUTER! SCAN FOR LIFE FORMS **BESIDES** US!
MY NAME IS NOT COMPUTER, IT IS AYA!
THERE ARE NO LIFE FORMS ABOARD THE SHIP EXCEPT YOURSELF, LANTERN KILOWOG AND LANTERN JORDAN.
BUT THEY ARE--
AYA CAN'T DETECT THEM, SO I THINK THIS GUY CONJURED THEM UP SOMEHOW...
...I DON'T THINK IT'S REAL! AND IF IT'S NOT REAL, IT WON'T MIND IF I DO THIS--
ARRGH!
KILOWOG?!!
NO!

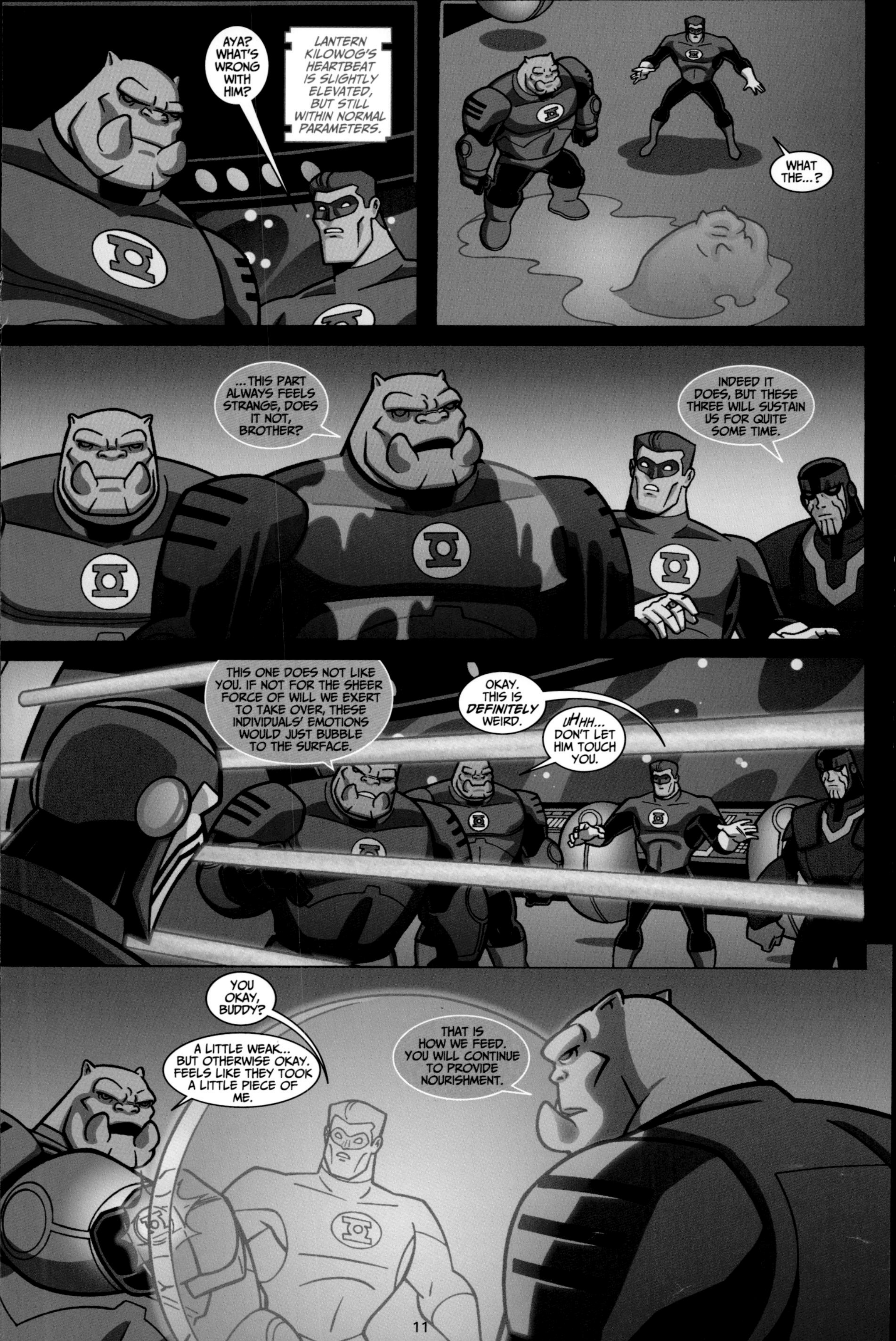
AYA? WHAT'S WRONG WITH HIM?
LANTERN KILOWOG'S HEARTBEAT IS SLIGHTLY ELEVATED, BUT STILL WITHIN NORMAL PARAMETERS.
WHAT THE...?
...THIS PART ALWAYS FEELS STRANGE, DOES IT NOT, BROTHER?
INDEED IT DOES, BUT THESE THREE WILL SUSTAIN US FOR QUITE SOME TIME.
THIS ONE DOES NOT LIKE YOU. IF NOT FOR THE SHEER FORCE OF WILL WE EXERT TO TAKE OVER, THESE INDIVIDUALS' EMOTIONS WOULD JUST BUBBLE TO THE SURFACE.
OKAY. THIS IS DEFINITELY WEIRD.
UHHH... DON'T LET HIM TOUCH YOU.
YOU OKAY, BUDDY?
A LITTLE WEAK... BUT OTHERWISE OKAY. FEELS LIKE THEY TOOK A LITTLE PIECE OF ME.
THAT IS HOW WE FEED. YOU WILL CONTINUE TO PROVIDE NOURISHMENT.

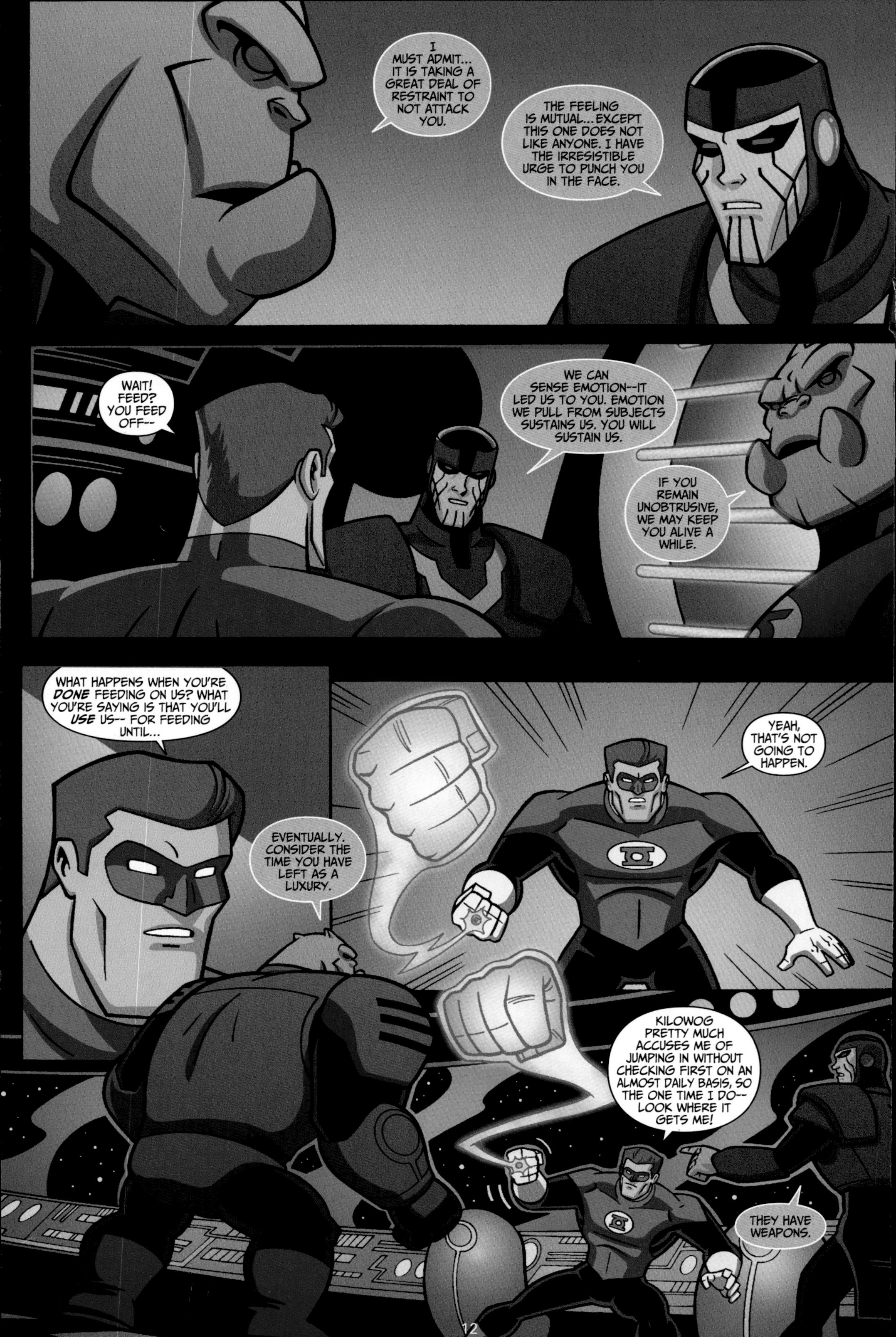
I MUST ADMIT... IT IS TAKING A GREAT DEAL OF RESTRAINT TO NOT ATTACK YOU.
THE FEELING IS MUTUAL... EXCEPT THIS ONE DOES NOT LIKE ANYONE. I HAVE THE IRRESISTIBLE URGE TO PUNCH YOU IN THE FACE.
WAIT! FEED? YOU FEED OFF--
WE CAN SENSE EMOTION--IT LED US TO YOU. EMOTION WE PULL FROM SUBJECTS SUSTAINS US. YOU WILL SUSTAIN US.
IF YOU REMAIN UNOBTRUSIVE, WE MAY KEEP YOU ALIVE A WHILE.
WHAT HAPPENS WHEN YOU'RE *DONE* FEEDING ON US? WHAT YOU'RE SAYING IS THAT YOU'LL *USE* US-- FOR FEEDING UNTIL...
EVENTUALLY. CONSIDER THE TIME YOU HAVE LEFT AS A LUXURY.
YEAH, THAT'S NOT GOING TO HAPPEN.
KILOWOG PRETTY MUCH ACCUSES ME OF JUMPING IN WITHOUT CHECKING FIRST ON AN ALMOST DAILY BASIS, SO THE ONE TIME I DO-- LOOK WHERE IT GETS ME!
THEY HAVE WEAPONS.

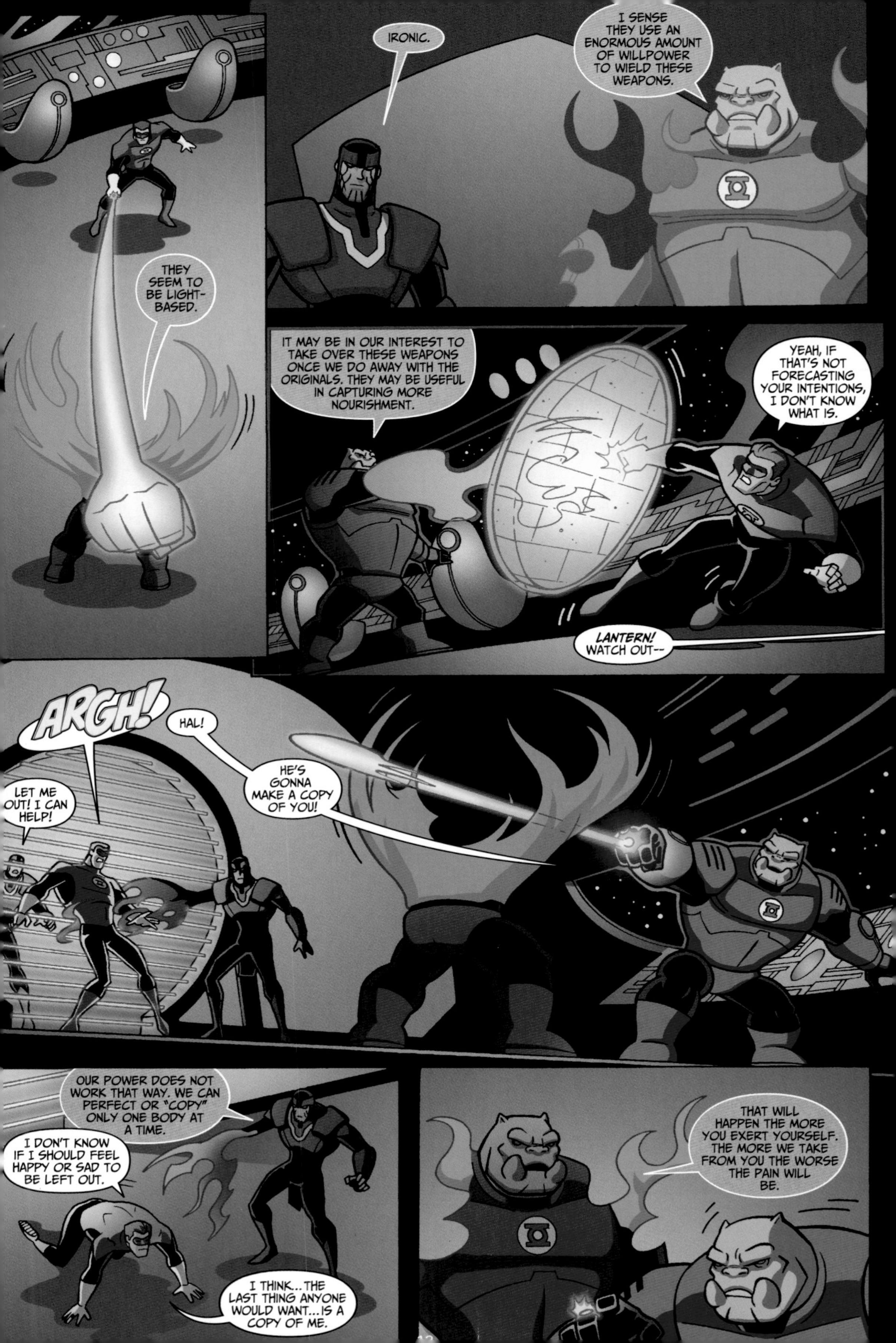

THEY SEEM TO BE LIGHT-BASED.
IRONIC.
I SENSE THEY USE AN ENORMOUS AMOUNT OF WILLPOWER TO WIELD THESE WEAPONS.
IT MAY BE IN OUR INTEREST TO TAKE OVER THESE WEAPONS ONCE WE DO AWAY WITH THE ORIGINALS. THEY MAY BE USEFUL IN CAPTURING MORE NOURISHMENT.
YEAH, IF THAT'S NOT FORECASTING YOUR INTENTIONS, I DON'T KNOW WHAT IS.
LANTERN! WATCH OUT--
ARGH!
HAL!
LET ME OUT! I CAN HELP!
HE'S GONNA MAKE A COPY OF YOU!
OUR POWER DOES NOT WORK THAT WAY. WE CAN PERFECT OR "COPY" ONLY ONE BODY AT A TIME.
I DON'T KNOW IF I SHOULD FEEL HAPPY OR SAD TO BE LEFT OUT.
I THINK... THE LAST THING ANYONE WOULD WANT... IS A COPY OF ME.
THAT WILL HAPPEN THE MORE YOU EXERT YOURSELF. THE MORE WE TAKE FROM YOU THE WORSE THE PAIN WILL BE.

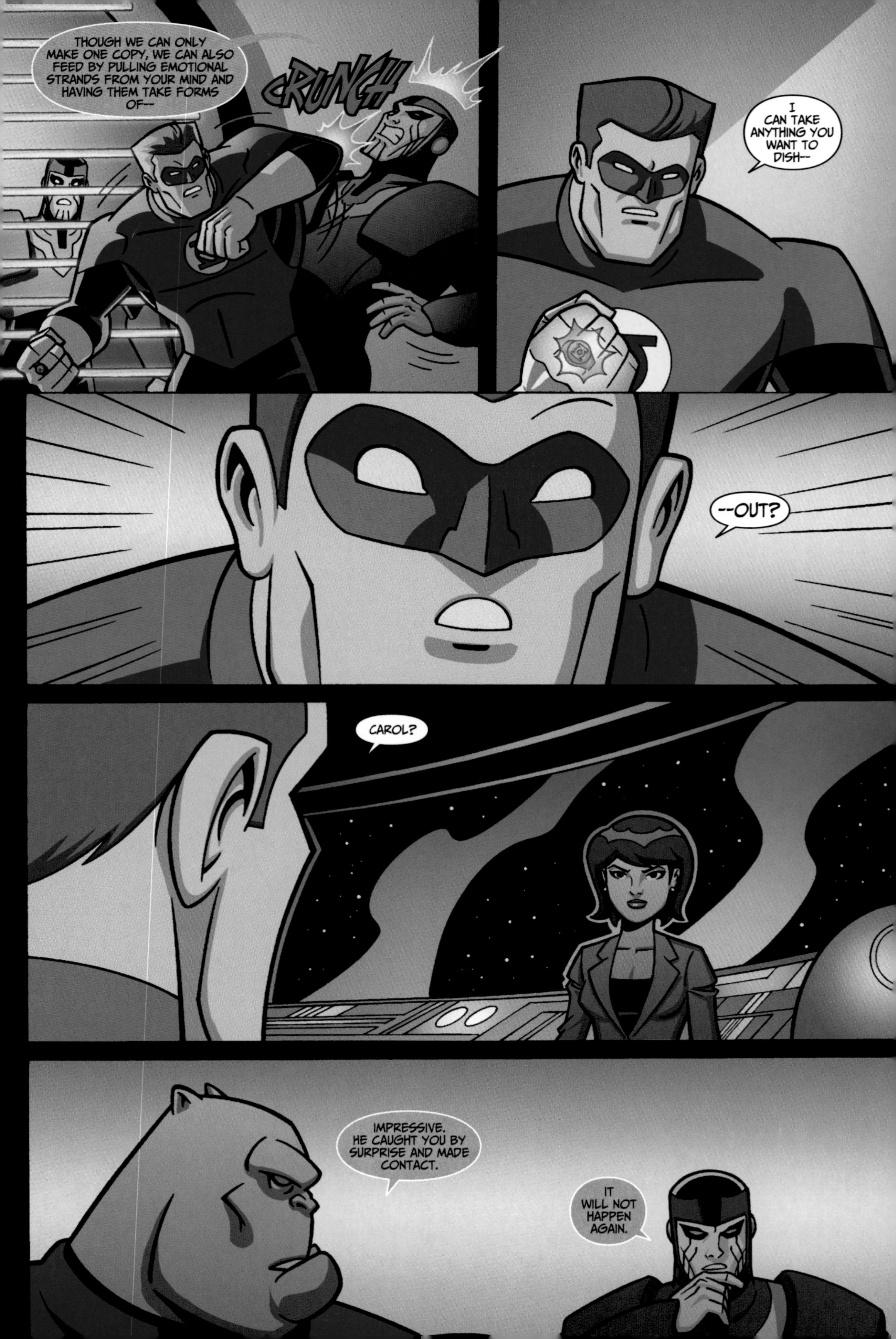
THOUGH WE CAN ONLY MAKE ONE COPY, WE CAN ALSO FEED BY PULLING EMOTIONAL STRANDS FROM YOUR MIND AND HAVING THEM TAKE FORMS OF--
CRUNCH
I CAN TAKE ANYTHING YOU WANT TO DISH--
--OUT?
CAROL?
IMPRESSIVE. HE CAUGHT YOU BY SURPRISE AND MADE CONTACT.
IT WILL NOT HAPPEN AGAIN.

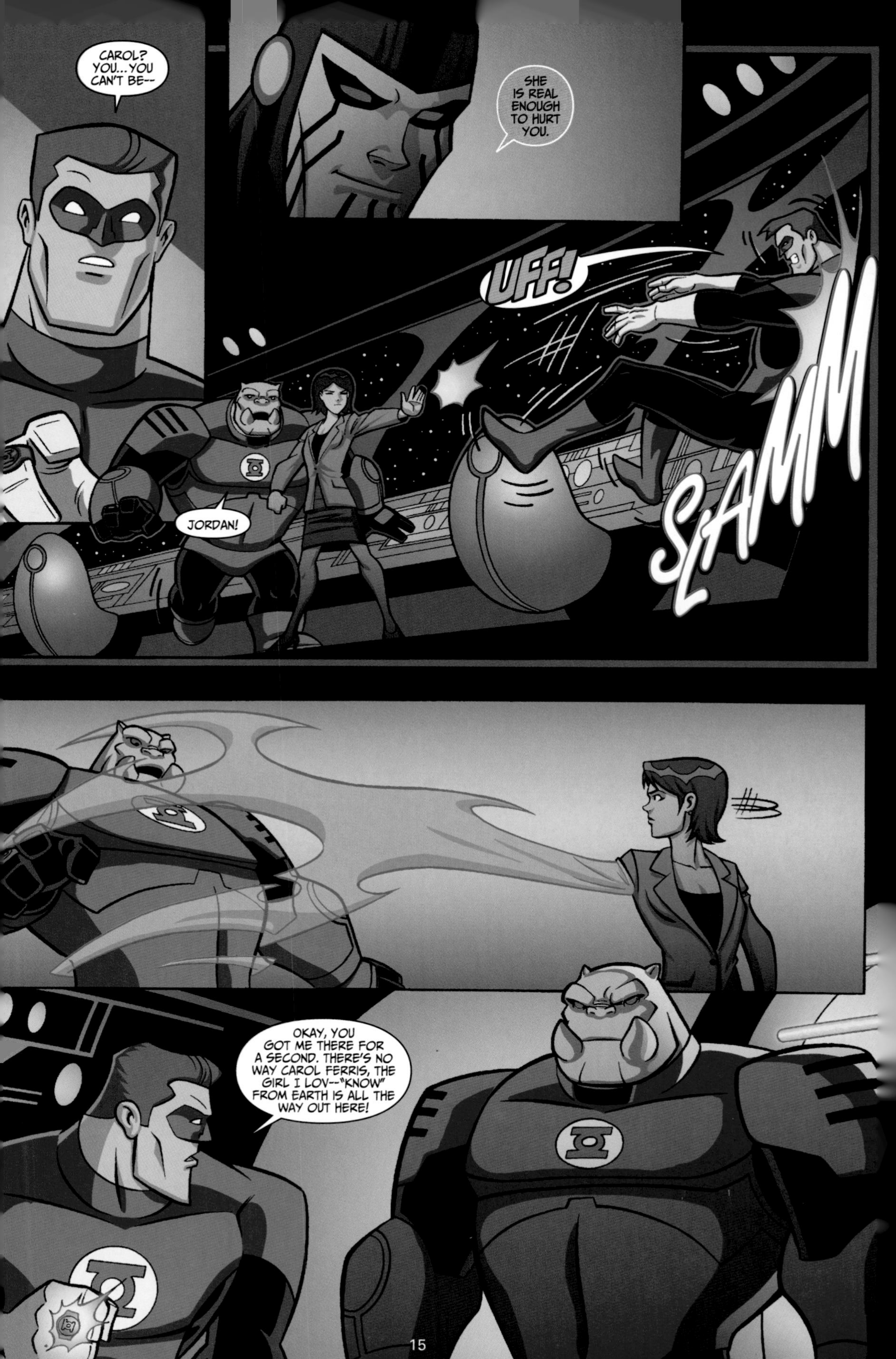

CAROL? YOU...YOU CAN'T BE--
SHE IS REAL ENOUGH TO HURT YOU.
UFF!
SLAMM
JORDAN!
OKAY, YOU GOT ME THERE FOR A SECOND. THERE'S NO WAY CAROL FERRIS, THE GIRL I LOV--"KNOW" FROM EARTH IS ALL THE WAY OUT HERE!

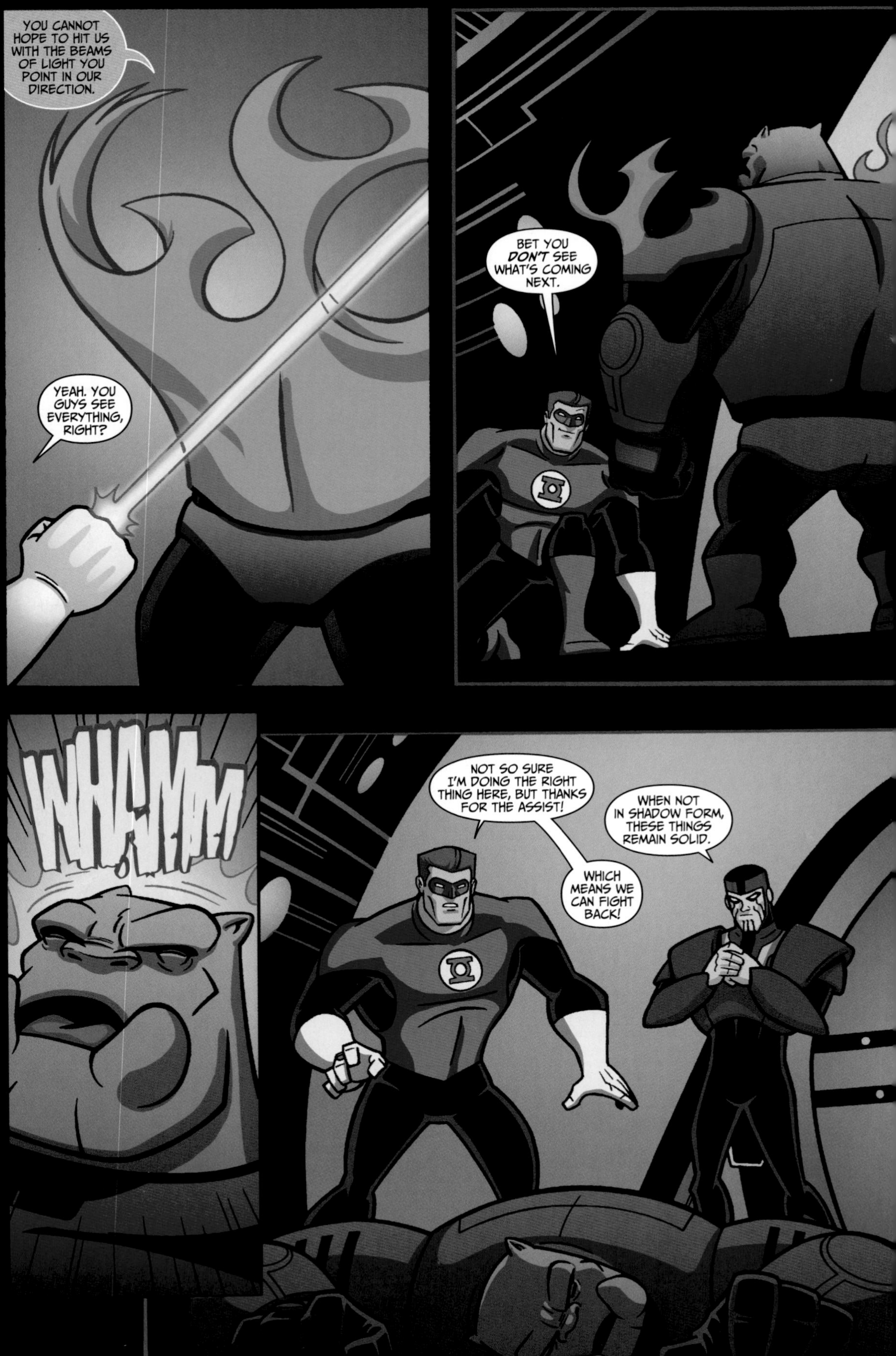
YOU CANNOT HOPE TO HIT US WITH THE BEAMS OF LIGHT YOU POINT IN OUR DIRECTION.
YEAH. YOU GUYS SEE EVERYTHING, RIGHT?
BET YOU DON'T SEE WHAT'S COMING NEXT.
WHAMM
NOT SO SURE I'M DOING THE RIGHT THING HERE, BUT THANKS FOR THE ASSIST!
WHEN NOT IN SHADOW FORM, THESE THINGS REMAIN SOLID.
WHICH MEANS WE CAN FIGHT BACK!

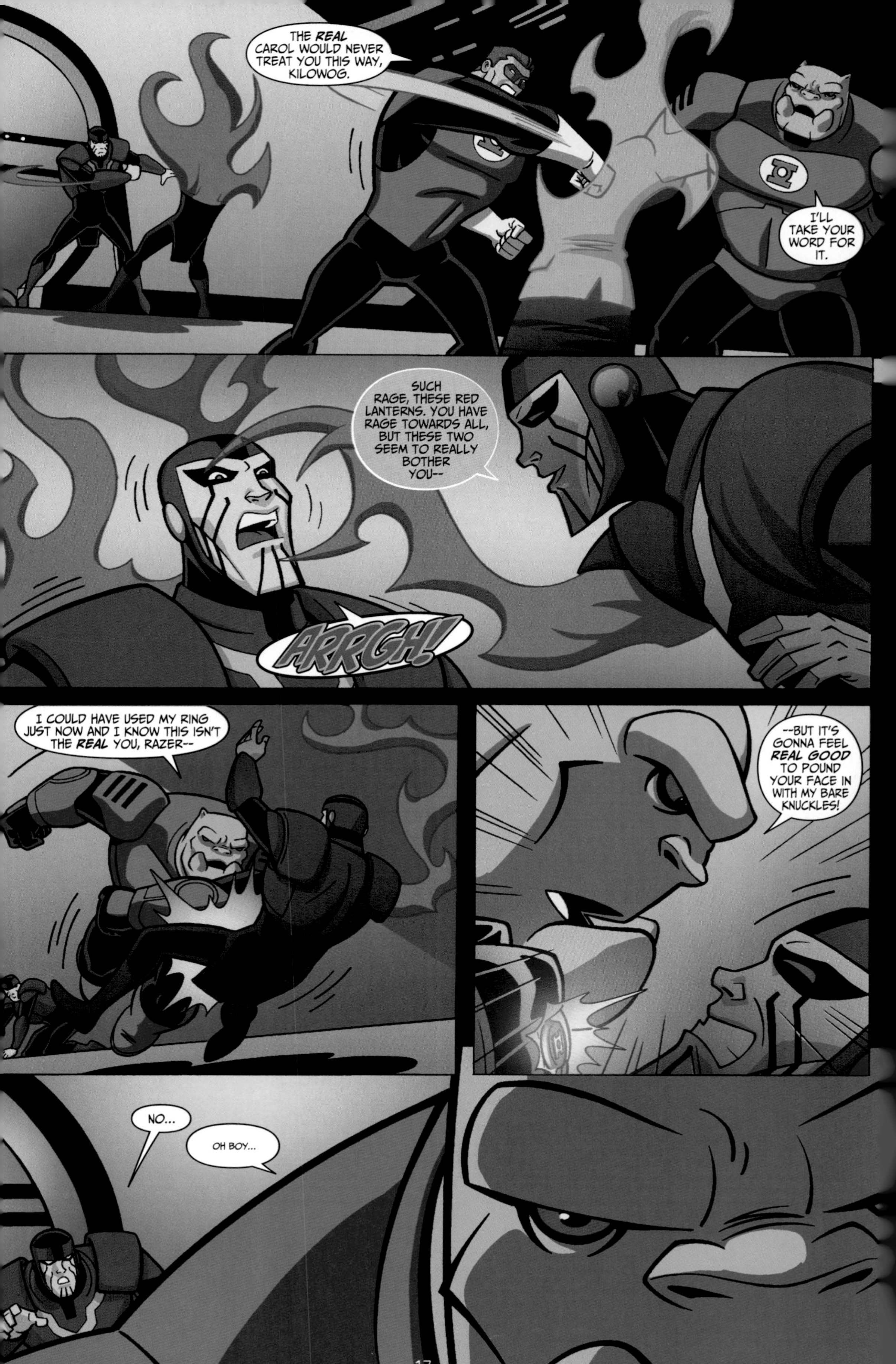
THE **REAL** CAROL WOULD NEVER TREAT YOU THIS WAY, KILOWOG.
I'LL TAKE YOUR WORD FOR IT.
SUCH RAGE, THESE RED LANTERNS. YOU HAVE RAGE TOWARDS ALL, BUT THESE TWO SEEM TO REALLY BOTHER YOU--
ARRGH!
I COULD HAVE USED MY RING JUST NOW AND I KNOW THIS ISN'T THE **REAL** YOU, RAZER--
--BUT IT'S GONNA FEEL **REAL GOOD** TO POUND YOUR FACE IN WITH MY BARE KNUCKLES!
NO...
OH BOY...

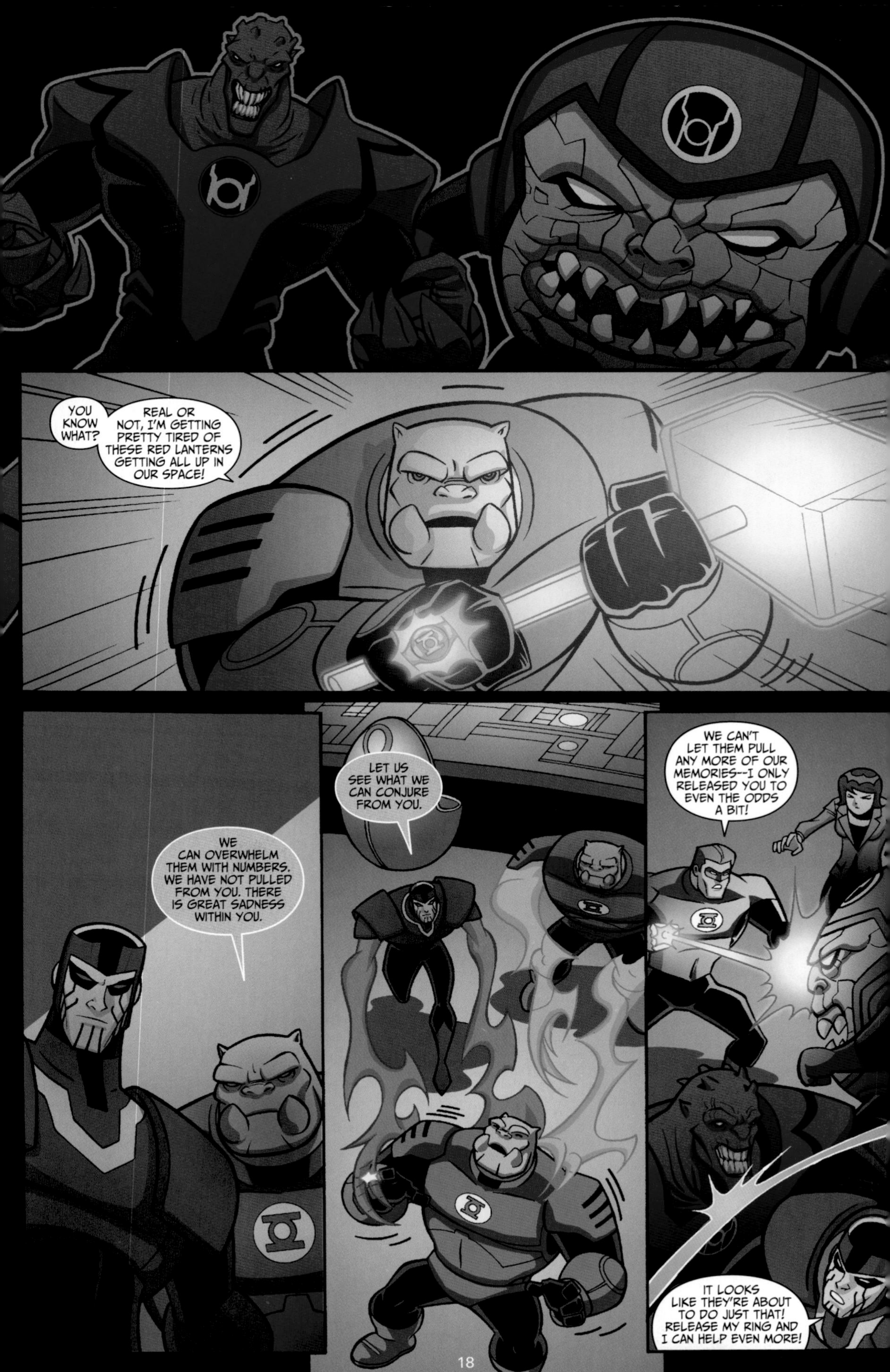
YOU KNOW WHAT?
REAL OR NOT, I'M GETTING PRETTY TIRED OF THESE RED LANTERNS GETTING ALL UP IN OUR SPACE!
WE CAN OVERWHELM THEM WITH NUMBERS. WE HAVE NOT PULLED FROM YOU. THERE IS GREAT SADNESS WITHIN YOU.
LET US SEE WHAT WE CAN CONJURE FROM YOU.
WE CAN'T LET THEM PULL ANY MORE OF OUR MEMORIES--I ONLY RELEASED YOU TO EVEN THE ODDS A BIT!
IT LOOKS LIKE THEY'RE ABOUT TO DO JUST THAT! RELEASE MY RING AND I CAN HELP EVEN MORE!

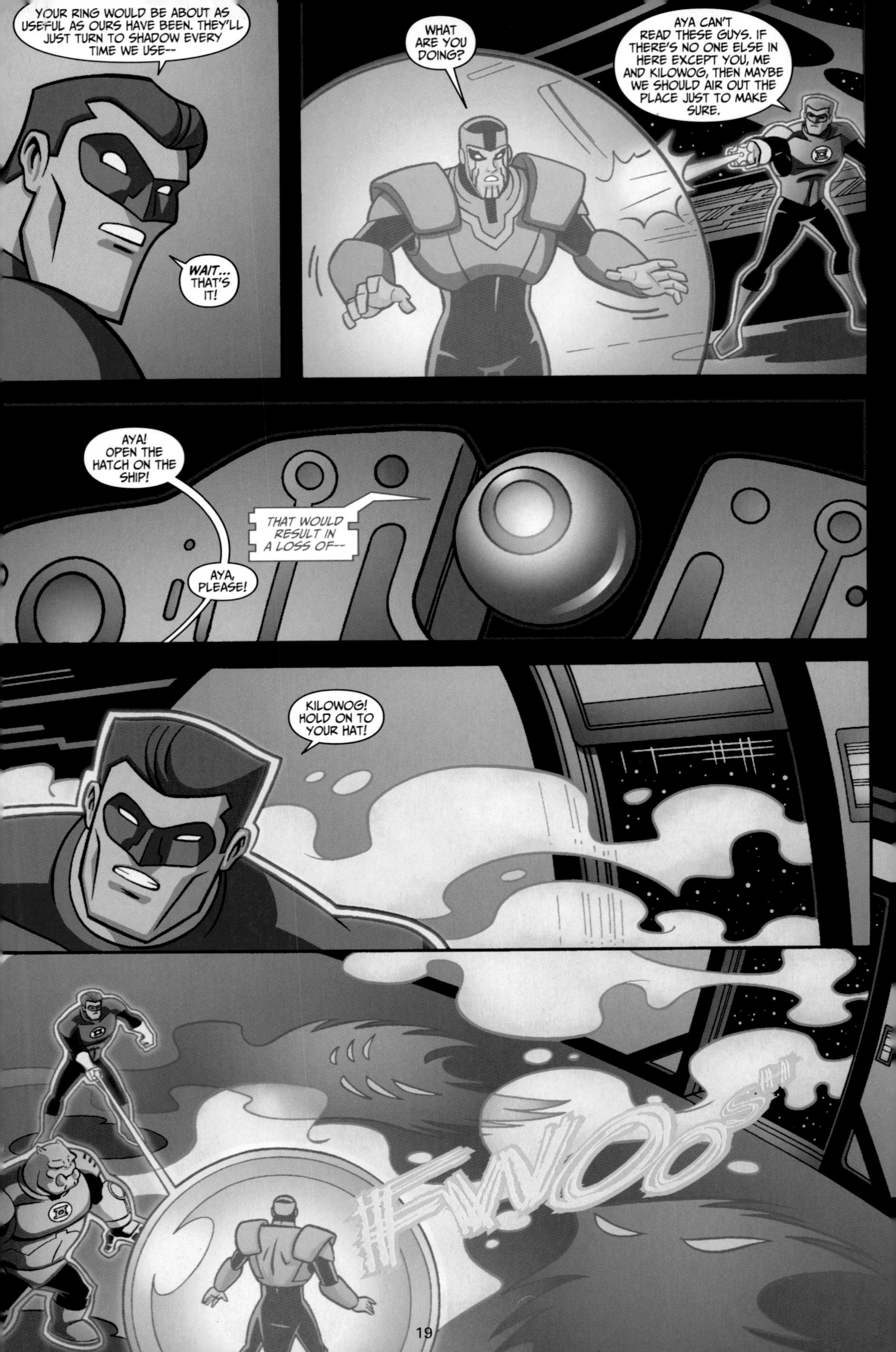
YOUR RING WOULD BE ABOUT AS USEFUL AS OURS HAVE BEEN. THEY'LL JUST TURN TO SHADOW EVERY TIME WE USE--
WAIT... THAT'S IT!
WHAT ARE YOU DOING?
AYA CAN'T READ THESE GUYS. IF THERE'S NO ONE ELSE IN HERE EXCEPT YOU, ME AND KILOWOG, THEN MAYBE WE SHOULD AIR OUT THE PLACE JUST TO MAKE SURE.
AYA! OPEN THE HATCH ON THE SHIP!
THAT WOULD RESULT IN A LOSS OF--
AYA, PLEASE!
KILOWOG! HOLD ON TO YOUR HAT!
FWOOSHH

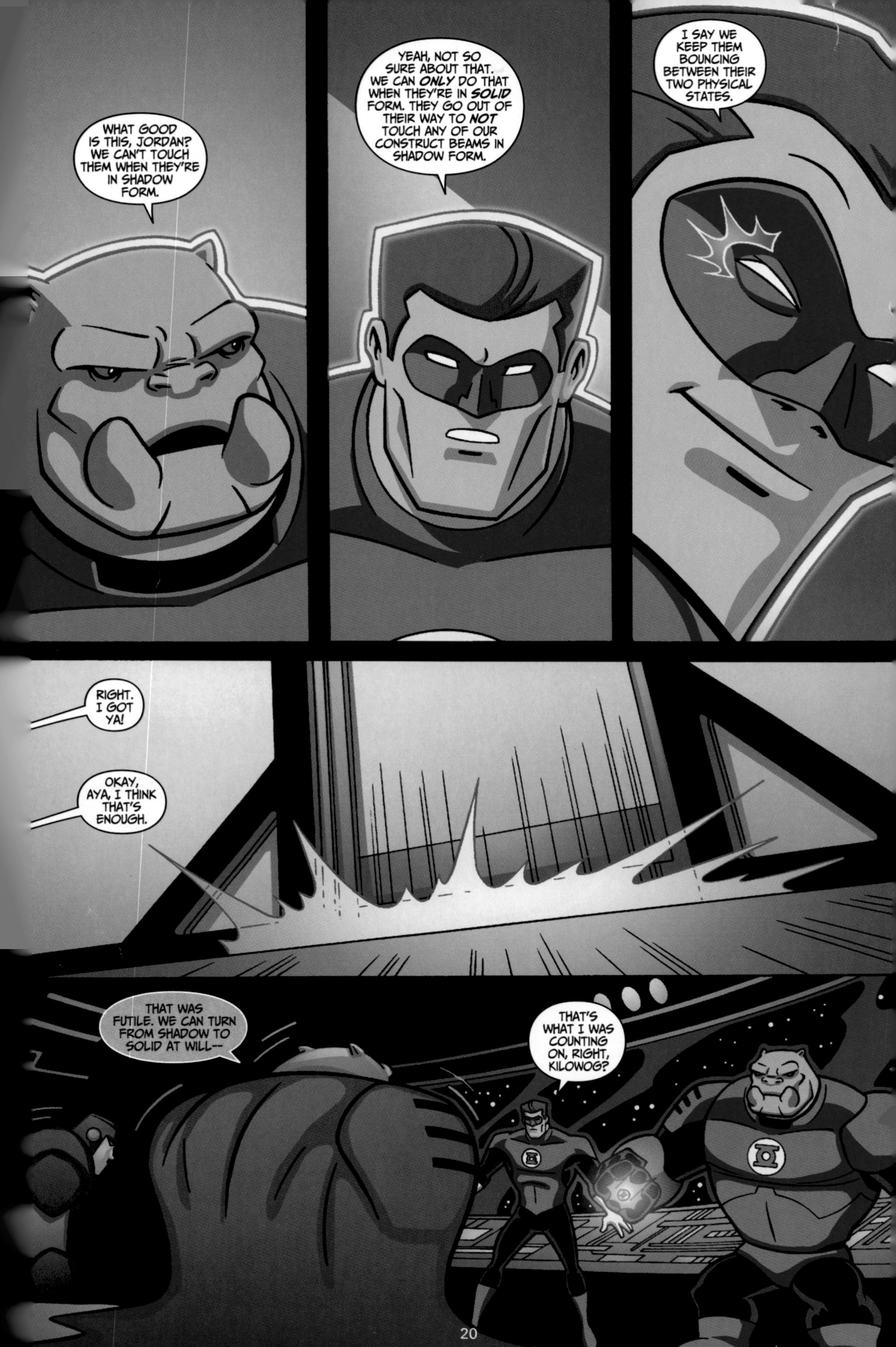
WHAT GOOD IS THIS, JORDAN? WE CAN'T TOUCH THEM WHEN THEY'RE IN SHADOW FORM.
YEAH, NOT SO SURE ABOUT THAT. WE CAN ONLY DO THAT WHEN THEY'RE IN SOLID FORM. THEY GO OUT OF THEIR WAY TO NOT TOUCH ANY OF OUR CONSTRUCT BEAMS IN SHADOW FORM.
I SAY WE KEEP THEM BOUNCING BETWEEN THEIR TWO PHYSICAL STATES.
RIGHT. I GOT YA!
OKAY, AYA, I THINK THAT'S ENOUGH.
THAT WAS FUTILE. WE CAN TURN FROM SHADOW TO SOLID AT WILL--
THAT'S WHAT I WAS COUNTING ON, RIGHT, KILOWOG?

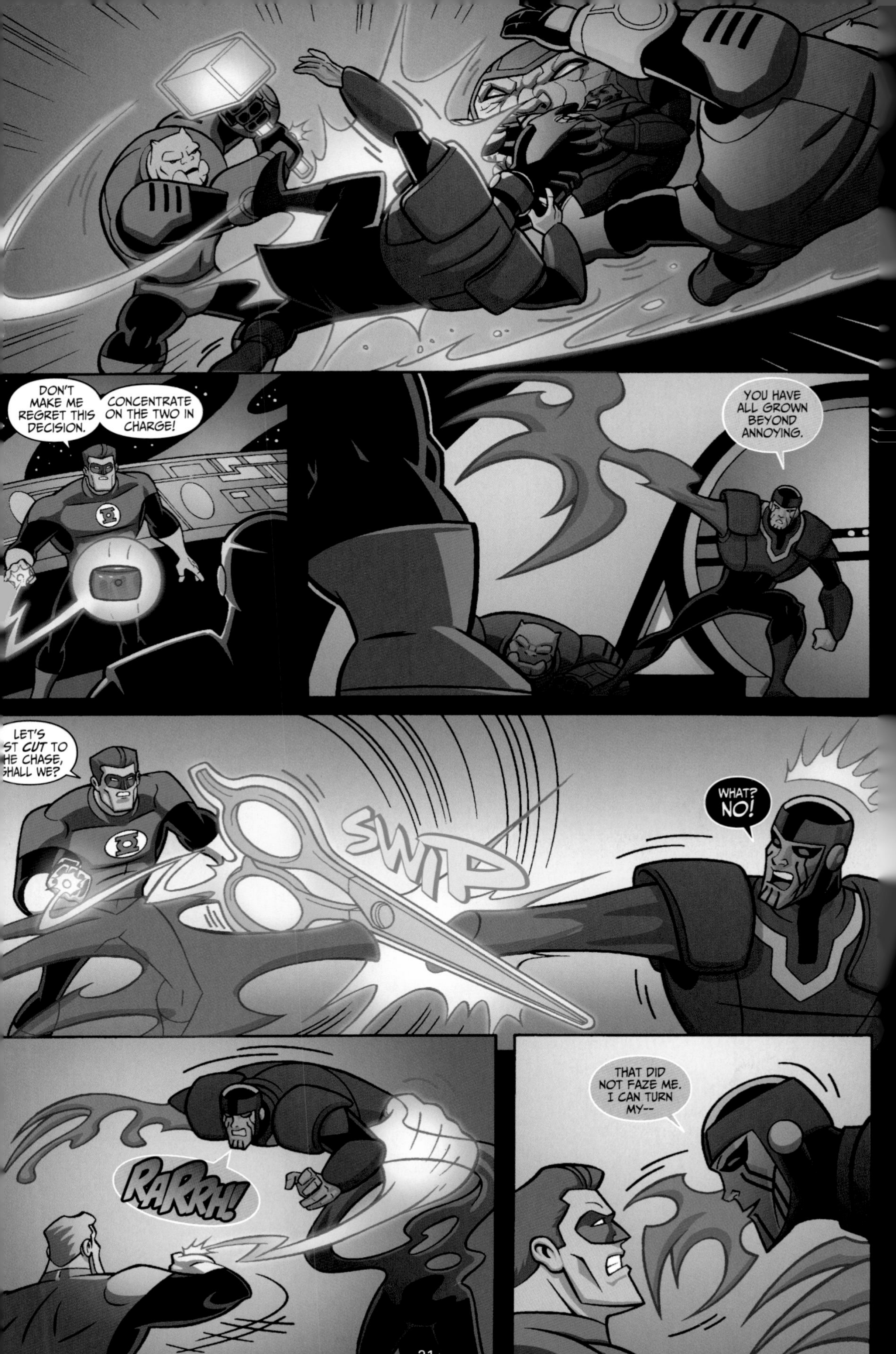
DON'T MAKE ME REGRET THIS DECISION.
CONCENTRATE ON THE TWO IN CHARGE!
YOU HAVE ALL GROWN BEYOND ANNOYING.
LET'S
ST CUT TO
HE CHASE,
HALL WE?
SWIP
WHAT? NO!
RARRH!
THAT DID NOT FAZE ME. I CAN TURN MY--

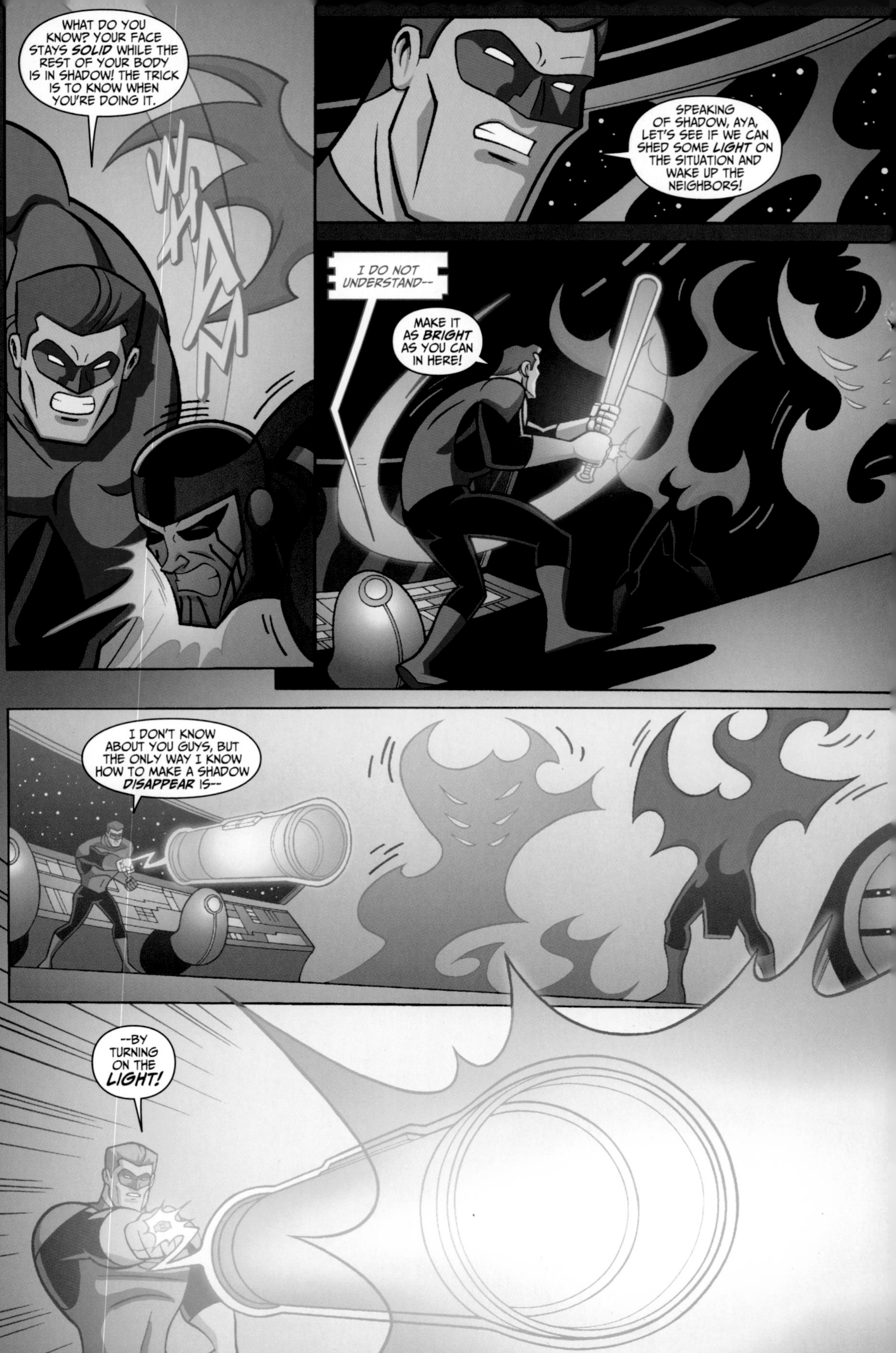
WHAT DO YOU KNOW? YOUR FACE STAYS SOLID WHILE THE REST OF YOUR BODY IS IN SHADOW! THE TRICK IS TO KNOW WHEN YOU'RE DOING IT.
WHAP
SPEAKING OF SHADOW, AYA, LET'S SEE IF WE CAN SHED SOME LIGHT ON THE SITUATION AND WAKE UP THE NEIGHBORS!
I DO NOT UNDERSTAND--
MAKE IT AS BRIGHT AS YOU CAN IN HERE!
I DON'T KNOW ABOUT YOU GUYS, BUT THE ONLY WAY I KNOW HOW TO MAKE A SHADOW DISAPPEAR IS--
--BY TURNING ON THE LIGHT!

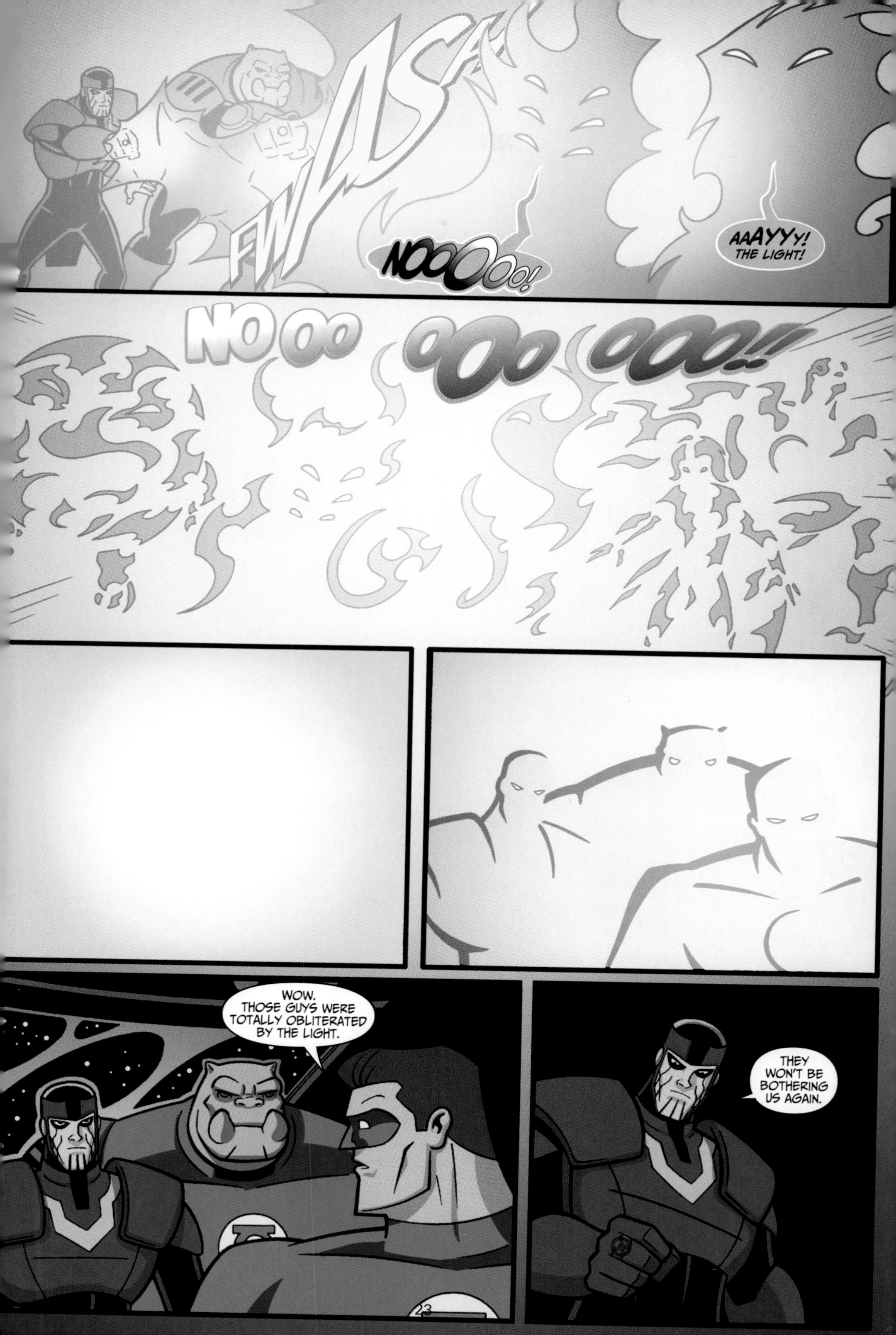
FWASA
NOOOOOO!
AAAYYy! THE LIGHT!
NOOOOOOOOO!!
WOW. THOSE GUYS WERE TOTALLY OBLITERATED BY THE LIGHT.
THEY WON'T BE BOTHERING US AGAIN.

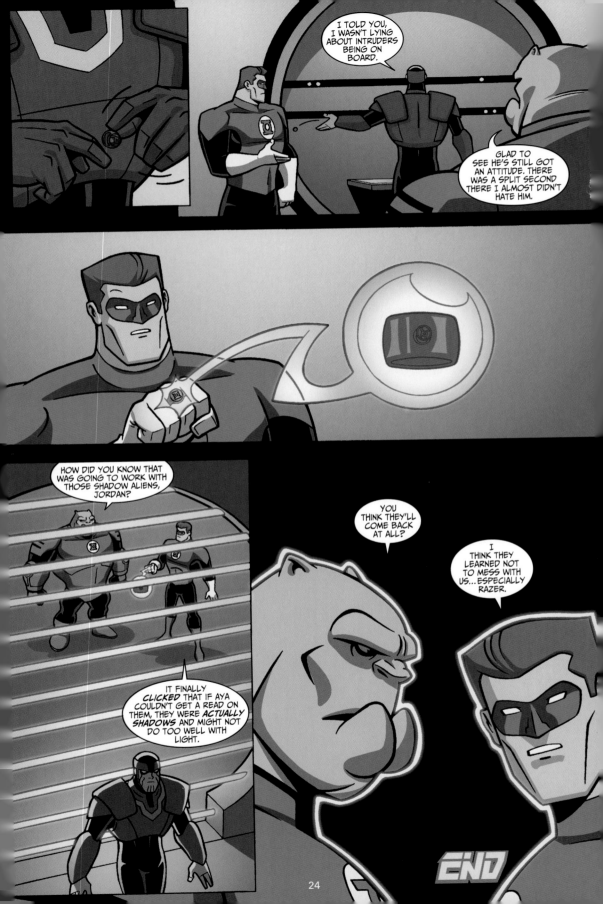

I TOLD YOU, I WASN'T LYING ABOUT INTRUDERS BEING ON BOARD.

GLAD TO SEE HE'S STILL GOT AN ATTITUDE. THERE WAS A SPLIT SECOND THERE I ALMOST DIDN'T HATE HIM.

HOW DID YOU KNOW THAT WAS GOING TO WORK WITH THOSE SHADOW ALIENS, JORDAN?

IT FINALLY *CLICKED* THAT IF AYA COULDN'T GET A READ ON THEM, THEY WERE *ACTUALLY SHADOWS* AND MIGHT NOT DO TOO WELL WITH LIGHT.

YOU THINK THEY'LL COME BACK AT ALL?

I THINK THEY LEARNED NOT TO MESS WITH US...ESPECIALLY RAZER.

END

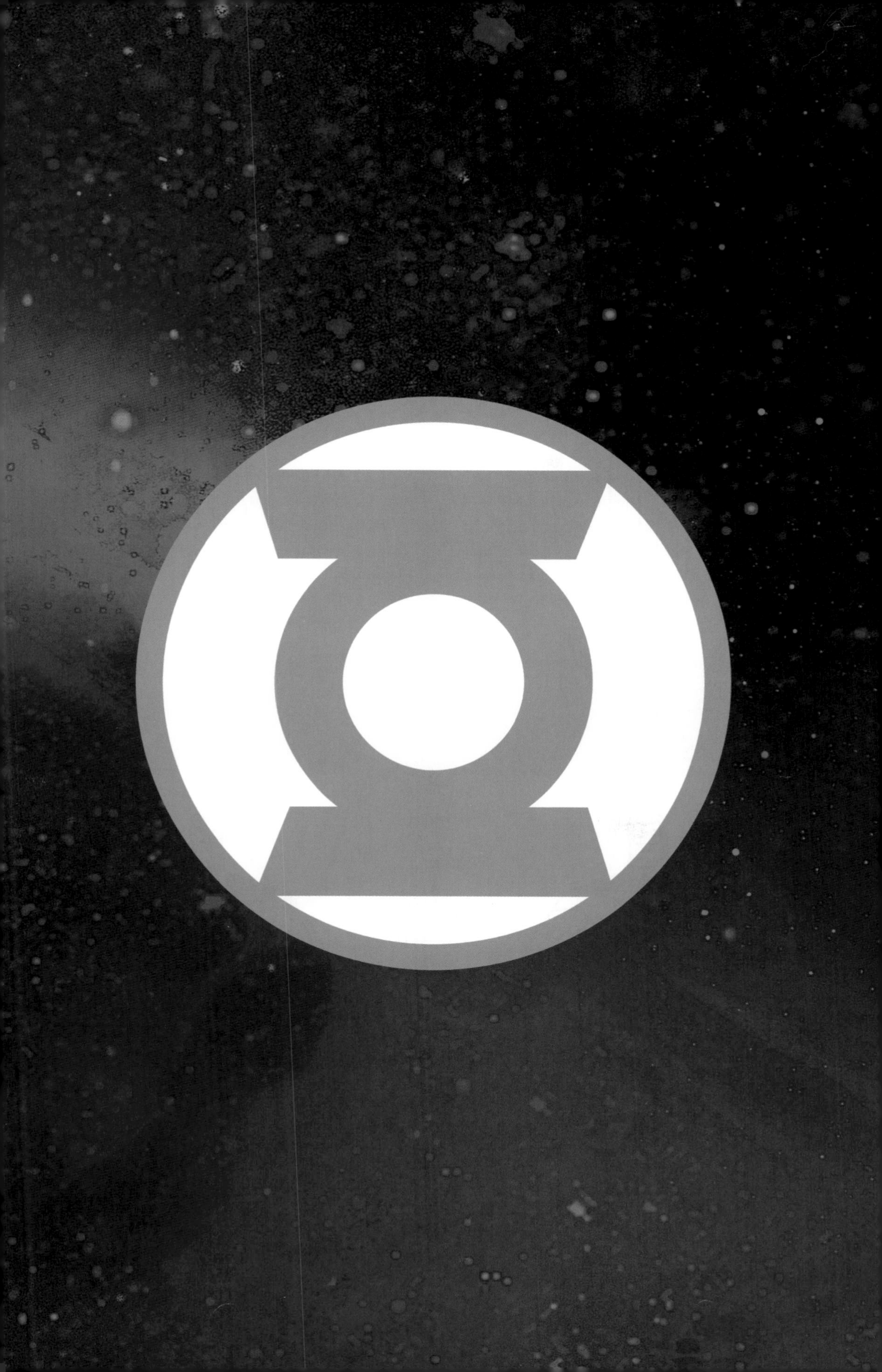

VISUAL QUESTIONS

1. On page 21, why did Hal Jordan return the Red Lantern ring to Razer? Do you think he made the right decision? Explain your answers using examples from the story.

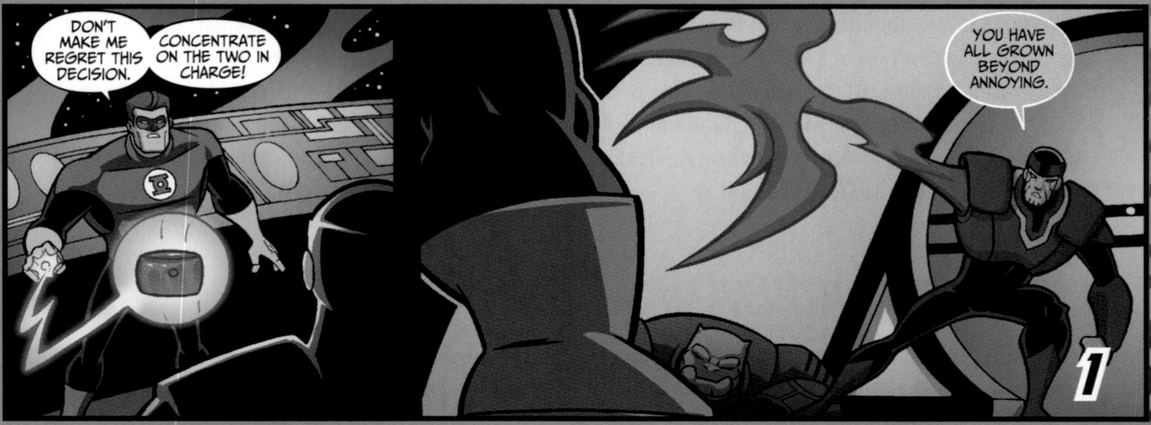

DON'T MAKE ME REGRET THIS DECISION.
CONCENTRATE ON THE TWO IN CHARGE!
YOU HAVE ALL GROWN BEYOND ANNOYING.

2. With his powerful green ring, Hal Jordan can create anything he imagines. If you wore a power ring, what would you create? Why?

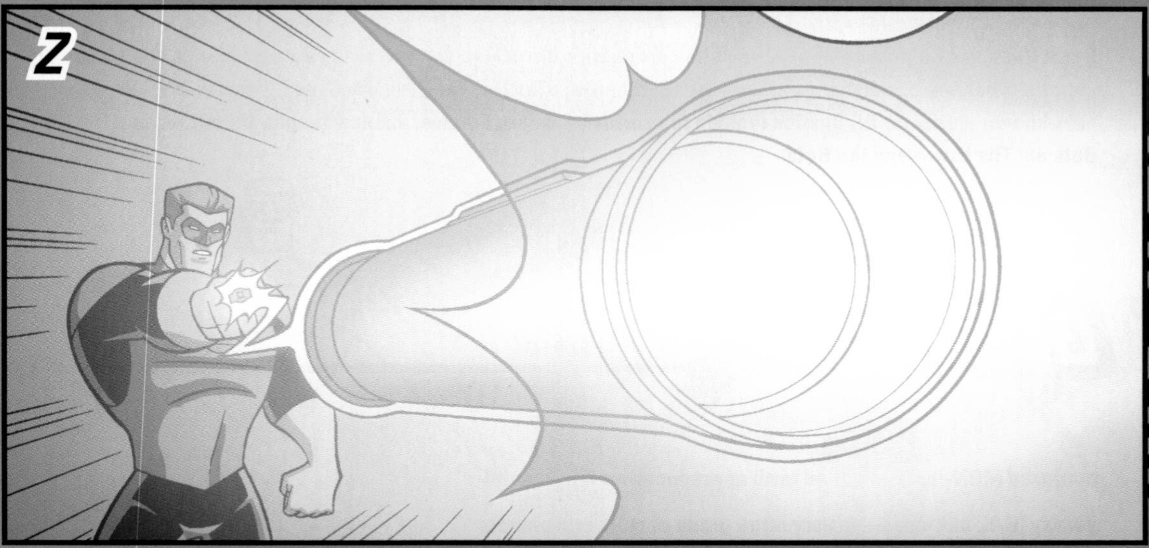

3. Based on the events in this story, do you think Razer can be trusted? Would you allow him to go free? Explain your answers.

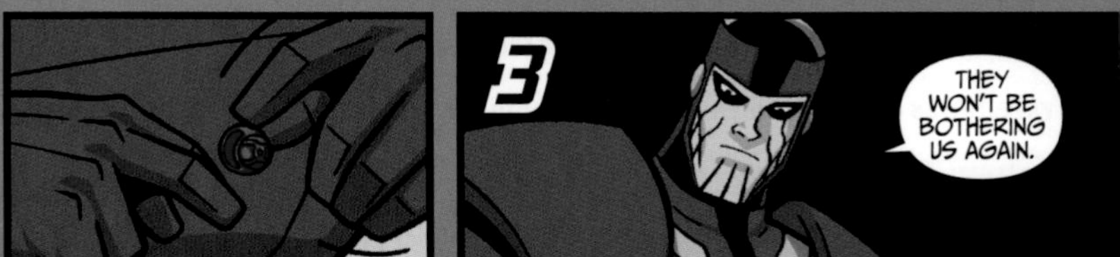

THEY WON'T BE BOTHERING US AGAIN.

4. In comic books, much of the story is told through the illustrations. Pick a page in this book, such as page 23, and rewrite the story using only words. Be sure to describe the setting, colors, and sounds!

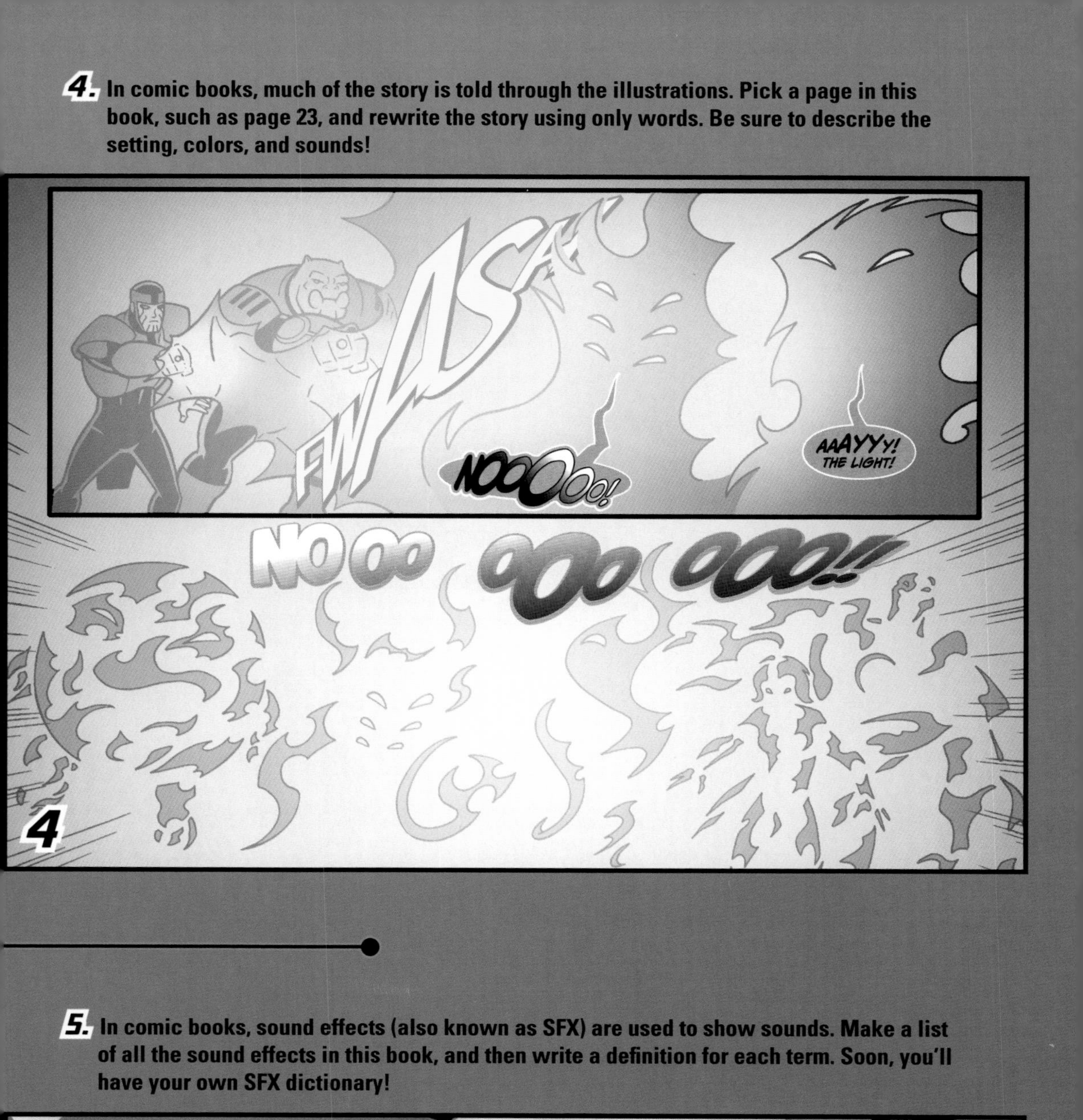
FWASA
NOOOOoo!
AAAYYy!
THE LIGHT!
NOOOOOOOOO!!
4

5. In comic books, sound effects (also known as SFX) are used to show sounds. Make a list of all the sound effects in this book, and then write a definition for each term. Soon, you'll have your own SFX dictionary!

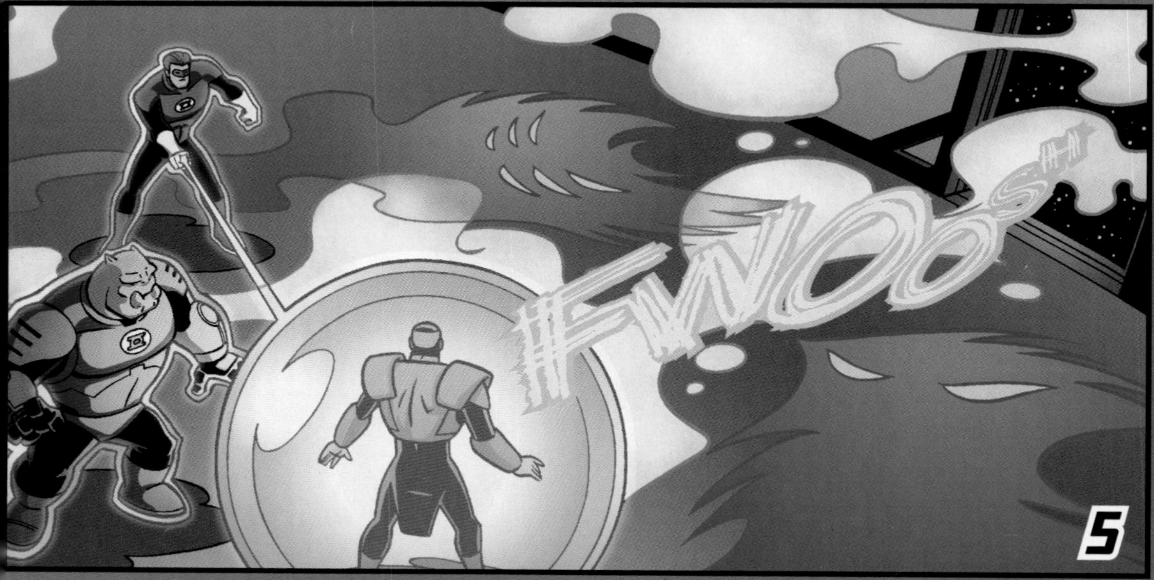
FWOOSH
5

READ THEM ALL!

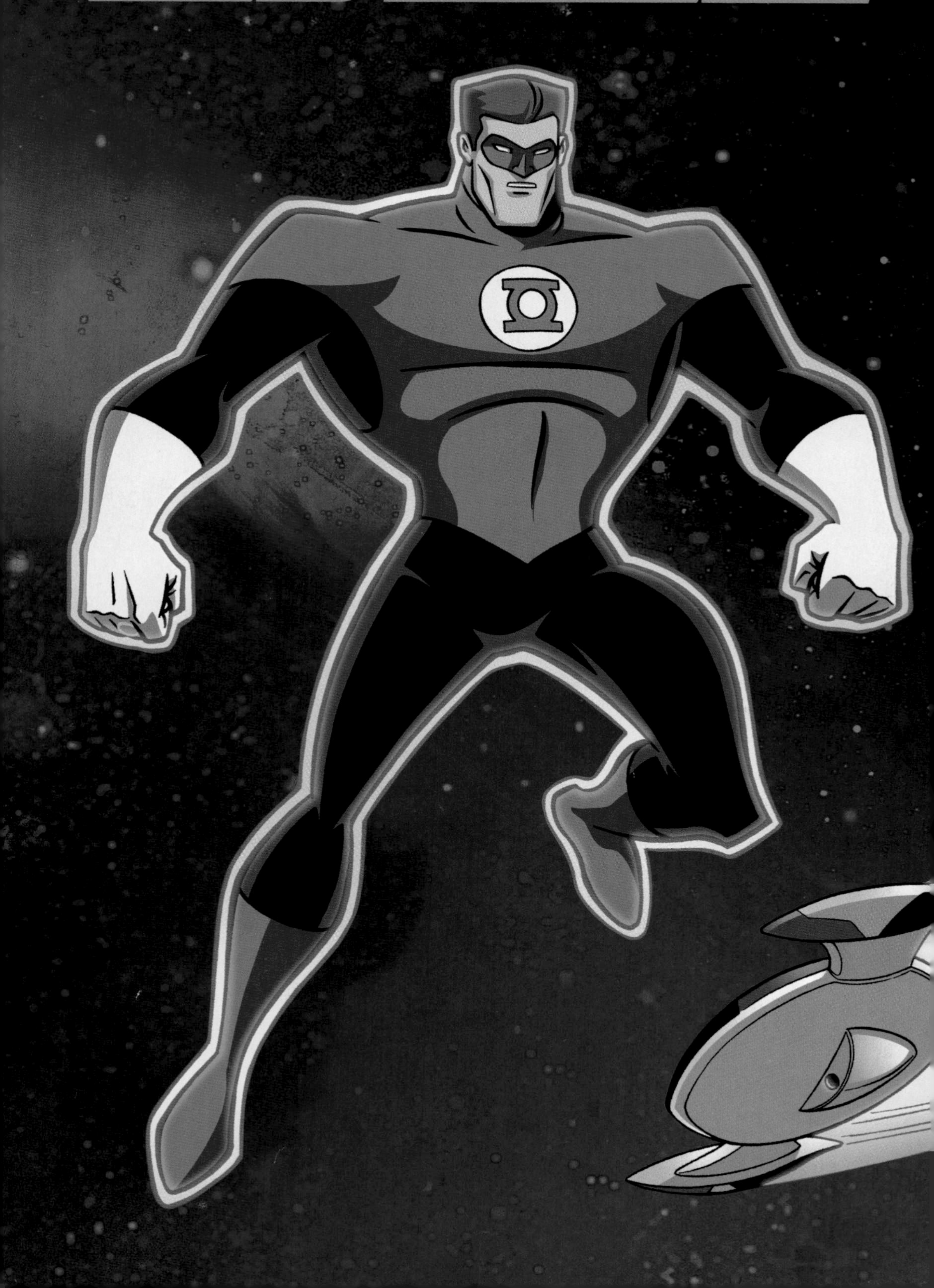

GREEN LANTERN
THE ANIMATED SERIES™
DC NATION
GREEN LANTERN THE ANIMATED SERIES
TRUE COLORS
BALTAZAR • FRANCO • BRIZUELA
DC NATION
GREEN LANTERN THE ANIMATED SERIES
THE INVISIBLE DESTROYER
BALTAZAR • FRANCO • BRIZUELA
DC NATION
GREEN LANTERN THE ANIMATED SERIES
SNIPER!
GOT HIM!
BOUNTY HUNTER
BALTAZAR • FRANCO • BRIZUELA
DC NATION
GREEN LANTERN THE ANIMATED SERIES
COUNTERFEITS
BALTAZAR • FRANCO • BRIZUELA
only from...
STONE ARCH BOOKS™
a capstone imprint www.capstonepub.com

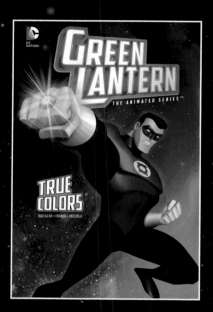

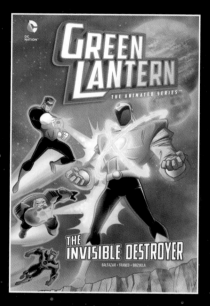

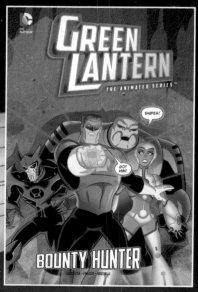

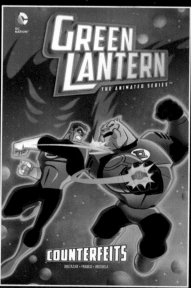

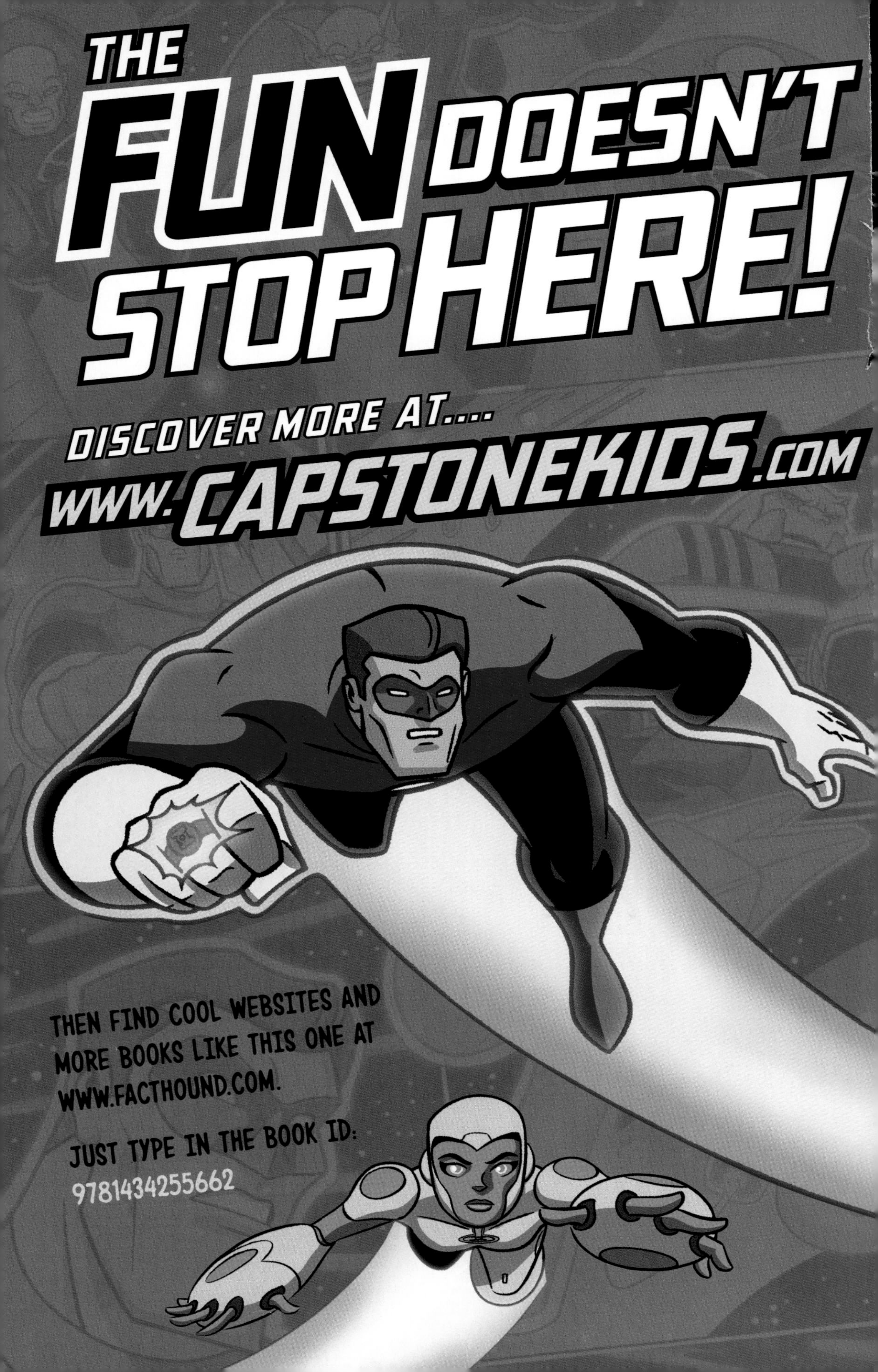
THE FUN DOESN'T STOP HERE!
DISCOVER MORE AT....
WWW.CAPSTONEKIDS.COM
THEN FIND COOL WEBSITES AND MORE BOOKS LIKE THIS ONE AT WWW.FACTHOUND.COM.
JUST TYPE IN THE BOOK ID:
9781434255662